Sew Sisters

I0681724

Stephanie Connors

ISBN 978-0-615-95288-8

Scripture quotations are taken from the King James Version of the Bible.

Unaware of the student chatter buzzing around her, Rebecca carefully scanned the community bulletin board for any available campus job. A paycheck was a must for getting her social life back in order. Happy hours and the latest fashion trends had depleted Rebecca's once comfortable savings account. Earlier in the year, Rebecca cashed in her meal cards to the University's bursar office just to make ends meet. These days making ends meet meant having enough money for the bucket specials at Tom's Tavern on Green Street. Almost compulsory to be a member of the student body, Rebecca joined the multitude who lined up around the block to partake in this Tuesday night ritual. The plastic buckets were filled with cheap draft beer and a stack of floating cups, a college delicacy that repeatedly drew a standing room only crowd.

Rebecca was determined not to let a lack of money hinder her good times. As she continued to search the board for job listings, a baby blue index card caught her eye. It read, **"Sew What?"** At first glance, Rebecca thought the heading was misspelled, but she continued to read just the same. **"Join us every Monday evening 6pm at 206 Albert Street for a time of friendship, sharing, and making new creations."**

As she read the card over again, a warm feeling flooded her whole body. She forgot temporarily about looking for a job and instead began to fish around in her backpack for her cell phone to enter the details from the card. Maybe she would drop in just once, she decided. Besides, there would still be plenty of time to catch up with her friends afterwards at their regular Monday night spot, Last Stop Dance Club. The dancing and drinking went on well past midnight so she felt assured she would not miss out on any action.

Amidst all the fun and frolic of college life, there was something missing inside Rebecca that she could not explain. After her freshman year, beer had officially become one of her main food groups, and she began to slowly lose herself in the whirl of activity.

Rebecca never intended to have the priorities that she had today. When she arrived on campus three years ago, she was a high energy, focused girl with big dreams of a career in journalism. Graduating near the top of her high school class, she placed great importance on grades and performance. She strived to be perfect in every way, putting endless effort into her academics as well as her extracurricular activities, dance and track. Even with the intensity with which she pursued her goals, Rebecca was never satisfied with her accomplishments.

Almost six feet tall, Rebecca caught other's attention easily with her strawberry blonde hair and vivid green eyes. Though Rebecca had many friends throughout high school, she never had a boyfriend. She felt safer having an ongoing crush on a boy who did not return her feelings. No chance of breaking up that

4

way. Her plan backfired when she had ended up with no date for prom. She put on a strong front to her family, but inside she was hurting for lack of a special companion. All and all, Rebecca survived the teen years with little drama.

Having never tried even a single drink of alcohol during high school, Rebecca wondered how she got to the place she was at now. No longer did her schedule center on classes, but instead her schedule revolved around being at the right party at the right time.

Deciding she needed a change, Rebecca typed into her calendar, "Monday, December 6th, 6pm, 206 Albert Street, Sew What?" The last time she had sewn anything was back in elementary school. Her mother had insisted Rebecca take two years of sewing at the local 4H club in her hometown. Maybe those years will finally come in handy next Monday, she reminisced. *Just maybe.*

2

Emma and Jake were married exactly five days when she knew she had made a bad decision. Ignoring her instincts, she agreed to marry Jake despite two years of a tumultuous relationship. The young couple wed in a small ceremony near Blackhawk Waterfall in Carillon Park. Just a few friends were in attendance, no family from either side. Emma figured it was their way of voicing their opposition by conveniently having other plans on their wedding day.

They honeymooned in Versailles, Kentucky, a two and a half hour drive from their two bedroom apartment in Kettering. A long weekend at Castle Post was the perfect setting to start their new life. Jake often indulged in luxurious get-a-ways, his way of trying to erase the episodes of trouble that seemingly came out of nowhere.

Now husband and wife, the two began what she had hoped to be a new chapter. But no sooner did Emma embark on this journey, did her life return to normal. Her normal, that is. On the drive home from their honeymoon, Emma suggested Jake slow down because his speed was making her both nervous and nauseas. He, in turn, sped up faster and took the next exit off the highway. He pulled into a convenience store and ordered her to get out of the car. He was not going to be told what to do.

Jake drove off. The car squealed out of the parking lot and back onto the road. Emma sat on the curb of the store front for a full hour until Jake returned. That was day five.

Ever hopeful, Emma pushed aside the incident and put her best effort into making their marriage work. She formally announced their nuptials by mailing beautiful cards with a wedding photo to family and friends. With the announcement, she had hoped to both reach out and mend fences with those she loved dearly. An occasional telephone call or card came in to congratulate the newlyweds. Emma cherished those connections, clung to them like a life line.

She had dreamed that marriage would be the answer to all she longed for in life. Instead, it only magnified the problems she had chosen to ignore the day she said, "I do." Excusing Jake's outbursts became routine. Nothing seemed to please him, and she grew weary trying. His anger came out in many forms and for reasons she could not track, let alone try to control. Over time, his temper grew progressively worse, becoming more violent and more personal with each episode. When throwing dishes and knick knacks could not satisfy his rage, he threw Bert. Emma trembled as she watched their helpless puppy hit the living room wall. "Stop!" she cried out. "Please!" Her plea only flamed his fury. He chased her into their bedroom, tackling her to the floor. Facedown in the carpet, he dragged her by her arm into their master bathroom. With one foot on her back to pin her, he squeezed globs of toothpaste in her hair. "You are a joke!" he said. He dropped her head and left.

Six months of marriage were six months of torment. Emma had lost all hope for change. Finding out she was pregnant woke her to the serious consequences of her choices. Emma instinctively knew she had to leave to protect herself and the baby. Broken-hearted, yet strong for her unborn, Emma plotted her escape. Jake's annual hunting trip was coming up and he was certain to be gone for a long weekend. The Monday after Thanksgiving was the start of buck season in Montgomery County. Jake and his buddies would leave at daybreak Saturday morning to get up to their usual cabin a few days early. This was her chance, her window for freedom.

She bid Jake goodbye that morning with the sweetest kiss, hoping her tenderness would shake off any suspicion. But he had no idea of her plan, or else he would never have left her alone. Emma waited two hours to make sure Jake had not forgotten anything and decide to return to the apartment. She knew the situation would be dangerous, even deadly, if Jake found her in the middle of the move. Though trembling with fear, she mustered up every ounce of her courage, packed a few belongings and left, hoping Jake would never make contact with her or their child.

Using the little cash she could access, Emma rented a small, but affordable condominium in Fairborn near the Parkway Mall. She had contacted the landlord in advance from an ad in the local newspaper. The landlord's name was Angela, but Emma lovingly teased that her name had to be misspelled.

"The 'a' at the end of your name must be a typo on your birth certificate," Emma said with a generous smile. "For you are an Angel to me!"

Angela was so helpful and kind. She understood the delicate situation and worked with Emma confidentially every step of the way. They had met in secret earlier in the week to take care of signing the lease and paying the deposit and rent. Angela gave her the key at that time so Emma would be ready for her escape.

She drove straight to Fairborn Commons, periodically looking up in the rear view mirror to make sure she was not being tailed. Once she arrived at the community, Emma was anxious to get inside her condominium. She quickly parked her car, took her keys, her purse, two small bags and her pillow and headed up to unit 2A. As she set her bags down to unlock the front door, Emma pulled out her cell phone to check the exact moment that marked her freedom. It was 11:58am, Saturday, November 27, 2011.

There she stood bombarded with emotions, feeling scared and alone, but released and free. When she opened the door to her new home, she shut the door to her old life. Inside, the quiet was deafening, strange and unfamiliar, but essential for her mind to sort through the decisions that were soon to follow. She soaked in the silence, like parched ground soaked in the rain. It was difficult for Emma to believe she was home and safe.

Suddenly she felt exhausted. With no furniture yet, she took her pillow and curled up on the floor in the corner of her living room. Before long, she was fast asleep. She slept for nearly two hours, oblivious of the thunderstorm that rolled through the area. Rain was unusual for November, but the temperatures were not cold enough for snow. The afternoon's storm was strong and loud, but Emma slept sound through it all, her body worn, her mind spent.

When she awoke from her nap, she felt rested, even peaceful. She decided to head to the Kroger to buy some groceries, reminding herself she was eating for two now. Strolling through the store, she was joyful thinking of the life growing inside her. She filled her cart with healthy fruits and vegetables and then headed to the check out. While standing in line, a colorful bulletin board by the customer service counter caught her attention.

After paying the cashier, Emma walked over to examine the board. She read through the various advertisements and flyers until a baby blue index card seemed to jump right out at her.

It read, **"Sew What?"** Interested, Emma silently continued reading. **"Join us every Monday evening 6pm at 206 Albert Street for a time of friendship, sharing, and making new creations."**

As she read the card through a second time, a warm feeling washed over her whole body. She could not afford to buy new things, but she could *make* them! She imagined sewing baby

11

outfits, blankets, and even curtains for her condominium. Without hesitation, she grabbed a pen off the service counter and scribbled down the details on the back of her store receipt.

I'll be there. Yep. This Monday, I will be there.

3

Pacing the floor, Bonnie wrestled hard with what seemed like never ending cravings of one kind or another. Just when Bonnie would walk out of the kitchen, prevailing over a particular desire, she would no sooner cave and walk right back in with a different fancy. Desserts were her weakness. Candy, cookies, cakes, pies, any and all desserts really. Night time was the worst, the time she was most vulnerable and most likely to binge. Tonight was no different.

After much angst and even more rationalization, Bonnie gave into the temptation figuring *tomorrow* was a good day to start her diet. She poured a glass of cold milk, pulled out an unopened cookie package and began to dunk one after the other. Standing at the counter, Bonnie polished off three dozen sandwich cookies in less than ten minutes, beating her previously held record of two and a half. Of course, she did not formally keep track of these statistics, but she could make a good guess, having stared many a night at the digital clock on the stove while she wolfed down her cookies of choice.

Bonnie had always struggled with her weight, starting in middle school. Her mother assured her that the extra inches were just baby fat and would disappear over time, but that never seemed to happen. Not to Bonnie's satisfaction anyway. She was tired of being described as "big boned" or "full figured."

She was never tired enough, though, to change her lifestyle for any real length of time.

Food was her comfort and always had been for as long as she could remember. Feelings of anger, sadness, and even joy brought her thoughts of different snacks and dishes. Recognizing her reasons for overeating did not help her. Rather the reasons became the legitimate excuses for breaking her diets over and over again. Thinking about food all day long was the norm for Bonnie.

No matter how much she willed herself to eat healthy, she seemed to have no control over her choices the minute something went wrong. Her problems, no matter how big or small, seemed to ease up with a plate or bowl in front of her. Ice cream was her favorite pacifier of all. Nothing compared to the texture and taste of chocolate peanut butter swirl, except for maybe chocolate chip cookie dough, or maybe caramel fudge delight or maybe chocolate chunk brownie. Yes, ice cream soothed her soul, unlike any other remedy she had experienced. Although she was never too successful at dating, Bonnie still held out romantic love to be the ultimate remedy and soul soother. In the meantime, she would stick with ice cream.

Bonnie had been an accountant at the CPA firm of Hanson, Bradford, and Skeen twelve years this past May. Her days were often long and stressful. She had been promoted twice during her employ as the partners valued her loyalty and meticulous work habits.

The office was designed in a typical cubical style. However, Bonnie's most recent promotion moved her to a small, but private office at the back right side of the payables' floor. Being a supervisor now, she was given charge over a department of ten employees. From behind her desk, she would issue her assignments, via email, of course. Face to face interaction was nothing but a nuisance for Bonnie.

She tolerated zero mistakes from herself and even less from her subordinates. Known for her strict and often callous direction, Bonnie's employees made no attempt to have any relationship with her besides a professional one. She was convinced that managing her career was entirely easier than managing her weight.

Bonnie kept her life uncomplicated. One day just followed the next with very little change. Even her weekends did not offer much in way of variety. Saturdays were for grocery shopping, laundry, and housework. Then Sundays, she would linger through the newspaper all day long with her two cats by her side, Missy and Barney.

Though she would never admit it out loud, Bonnie wanted to marry, raise a family, and live happily ever after. But when that dream would rise up, she remembered achieving it would require getting a boyfriend first, and then she would quickly toss that dream to the side. Sure, Bonnie had boyfriends in the past, but they did not seem to stay boyfriends long. Believing a man could love her for who she was on the inside seemed impossible to

Bonnie. Deep down, she felt bad about how she looked and was afraid to date. Worse, she felt too bad to do anything about her insecurity. It was just simpler to rent a movie and pop candied malt balls than to chance another relationship.

Early one morning in late November, Bonnie sat propped up in bed leafing through the Dayton Herald like any typical Sunday, when a certain advertisement drew her attention in the classified section. It read, **"Sew What?"** Curious, Bonnie read further, **"Join us every Monday evening 6pm at 206 Albert Street for a time of friendship, sharing, and making new creations."**

Intrigued, she decided to read the ad through a second time. As she read, a warm feeling wrapped around her whole body. A renewed sense of hope began to fill her thoughts. She imagined herself in a new wardrobe and in a new size. She tingled all over thinking of designs and styles created for a new trimmed down self. Lately, Bonnie had become so comfortable with depression that any amount of excitement caused her to retreat. But somehow this excitement was different. She gravitated towards the adventure instead of running away.

She did not stop and question her response; rather she grabbed her appointment book from off the night stand, wrote down the details from the ad on the December 6th block, and made a silent promise to be there. *The time has come. My time has come.*

4

Lights out at 10pm was the rule, no exceptions. Maggie never imagined she would ever tuck her children in at a homeless shelter. She held tight to their good night routine. Rocking them, telling a favorite story, and then kissing them sweetly on the cheek. Even in the middle of their mess, bedtime remained the most precious moment of her day.

Maggie tried to sleep, but instead laid awake in the bottom bunk, listening to the rustling about in the dark room. Women in one room with the children, men in another room down the hall. Good sleep was hard to come by these nights. Meanwhile the mornings came early at the Chrysalis Center for the Homeless. Chores to be done, meetings to attend, jobs to seek.

"Good morning, Chrysalis residents!" greeted the anonymous voice over the intercom at 6am each new day, including Sundays.

Less than six months ago, Maggie and Matt Tucker lived in a beautiful four bedroom home in Hickory Hills, a new subdivision complete with a community pool and all the frills. They seemed to have it all, or at least what most people ascribed to having it all.

When Matt lost his job as a project manager, they fell behind on their mortgage. To help get current, Maggie picked up extra hours at the Macon paper company where she worked as a senior customer service representative. Matt did odd jobs on weekends for neighbors and furiously filled out applications Monday through Friday. Overqualified for most positions, Matt would have taken anything that remotely came his way.

Trying to refinance was now next to impossible on their reduced household income. Besides, they owed significantly more than their home was valued, complicating matters even more. The buzz term was that the Tucker's home was 'under water'. Maggie thought the term was perfect, as she and her husband felt trapped under water, drowning emotionally as well as financially. Originally hoping to save their home, they made the hard decision to list it with a realtor. A short sale would have been the best outcome at this point. But that never happened. Instead the bank foreclosed, and the Tuckers now called the Chrysalis Center home.

Part of living at the center meant regular participation in group and individual activities. Maggie and Matt were mainly interested in the Life Skills classes. Though compulsory, the topics seemed fun and applicable. A sixty day stay mandated a minimum of three different Life Skills classes per week. The couple carefully read the handout that outlined the course selections, the majority focusing on money and jobs.

Matt signed up for Financial Management and Interviewing Techniques as his first and second pick. His third class would be Positive Parenting which he would take together with his wife. Maggie was encouraged to take practical classes such as Time

Management and Banking Basics, but her heart really wanted to take the home making courses. She was determined to make a home once again for their family. To help keep a bright outlook on their future, Maggie chose hope over practicality. She signed up for Positive Parenting with Matt, along with Cooking with Care, described as nutritional basics on a budget.

With just one course left to choose, Maggie spotted a class called **"Sew What?"** Curious, she read on, **"Join us every Monday evening 6pm at 206 Albert Street for a time of friendship, sharing and making new creations."**

She read the description through a second time. As she read, a warm feeling engulfed her whole body. Her heart soared as she pictured sewing bedding and curtains and other beautiful treasures for their new home. The first class was tomorrow night. At once, she hurried to the sign up sheet at the front desk and listed her three choices. Afterward, she hustled upstairs to her quarters and marked the dates with the time and location of each class on her personal wall calendar that hung next to her bunk.

She sat on the edge of her bed and continued to visualize things she could sew for their home, crediting her day dreams to keeping her sane. *Tomorrow night. She would rebuild their life, day by day, stitch by stitch.*

5

Anna enjoyed brushing her long hair out every evening before turning into bed. Restful sleep came easy to her, a gift from the good Lord she always appreciated. *"...for so he giveth his beloved sleep." Psalm 127:2* Though a widow now more than three years, Anna remained content to sleep on her side of the bed. Like a wave, memories of her beloved husband sometimes knocked her over without warning. The waves of grief have grown fewer and farther apart now, but she will always love Samuel.

Samuel was a wonderful husband. It was effortless for Anna to return his love. Their commitment to one another did not waiver through good times or bad, sickness or health, even richer or poorer. Sure, they had their problems. But nothing was too big for God who was at the center of their relationship. Their covenant with God was stronger than any trouble that came against them. *"For with God nothing shall be impossible." Luke 1:37*

Anna had just celebrated her sixty second birthday when Samuel went home to be with the Lord. Never expecting to be a widow this soon, Anna desired to live out the rest of her life helping others. She prayed that God would reveal her calling in this new stage of her life. *"The eyes of your understanding being*

enlightened; that ye may know what is the hope of his calling..."
Ephesians 1:18

Finding more time on her hands now, Anna resumed her hobby of sewing. She loved to sew when her children were young. Being a full time mom and homemaker was her dream. She stayed home with them before school age only taking a part time job once they both entered kindergarten. As the children grew, so did her schedule. She found that sewing took a backseat to youth group, baseball, dance lessons, and Karate.

Starting a sewing group in her home was an ideal way for Anna to renew her hobby and reach out to the community. She was so excited about her decision that she began to advertise her upcoming class.

Sew What?

Join us every Monday evening 6pm at 206 Albert Street for a time of friendship, sharing and making new creations.

Local establishments were eager to allow Anna to post her ad on their community bulletin boards. And the Dayton Herald offered exceptionally reasonable advertising rates striving to boost their readership. With wheels in motion now, lessons would soon be under way.

6

Sunday afternoon, Rebecca woke with her usual hangover following a late night out with friends hopping house parties in the off campus neighborhood just bordering the University. Rebecca had just promised herself that Friday night was to be the last time she ever drank, ever. She broke that promise as soon as her roommate Eve texted her about a fraternity party happening Saturday night, the house within walking distance to her apartment. Frat parties were her favorite. Never a cover charge for girls and never an empty keg. Perfect for her wages and perfect for her non-stop plan for fun.

Unpacking the few belongings she managed to leave with, Emma looked around her new surroundings and appreciated the stillness of her new home. Free from Jake, free from abuse. She feared the peace was just temporary, but decided not to dwell on that possibility for the moment. It may only be a matter of time before Jake comes to find her. Emma pushed those thoughts aside and focused on emptying suitcases and boxes. She was tired and worn, and in much need of both physical and emotional rest. The image of holding her baby kept her going as she pressed on through the evening resolved to setting up home, sweet, home.

After Bonnie exhausted the newspaper cover to cover, she spent the rest of her Sunday afternoon daydreaming in her recliner. Tomorrow was Monday, her usual day to begin a new diet. She contemplated the different diets currently the fad. Each one offering a better promise than the next.

Convinced none of these familiar plans worked, Bonnie planned to take this coming week to research her options. The *following* Monday would be her start date for sure. With that decided, Bonnie figured she might as well eat hearty tonight knowing a week from now she would be starting a new diet, a serious one at that.

———————

Following Sunday's evening dinner in the Chrysalis Dining Hall, Maggie and Matt quickly did their assigned chore of taking out all kitchen garbage to the dumpster. Tasks rotated regularly between families and included the duties of cooking, cleaning, dishes and trash.

At each meal, the residents and their children sat together at long tables in a common gymnasium type room. After clean up, the families would usually rest where ever they could find a bit of privacy in small living room arrangements scattered throughout the building. Grateful to have a place to eat and sleep, Maggie and Matt tried to shield their children from the worries that consumed them privately.

During family time, Maggie shared her excitement with Matt about her upcoming sewing class. Matt was happy to see Maggie's enthusiasm and encouraged her to go without any reservations.

Maggie explained she would buy the material for her class from the donation store located within Chrysalis. The on site store was filled with community outreach donations that ranged from clothing to shoes to household items. Residents could shop with "Homeward Bound Bucks." These "Bucks" were earned for such behaviors as following rules, attending classes, completing chores and helping others succeed. Maggie had at least fifty dollars in "Homeward Bound Bucks" tucked away and had spotted some beautiful fabric at the store on her last visit. Maggie would put her hard earned "Bucks" to good use, glad she saved them for such an occasion.

7

Anna loved her wedding day! It could not have been more perfect. She had all she ever hoped for on their blessed occasion. Beautiful weather, family and friends, but most of all, Samuel. They were best friends through thirty five years of marriage. Love and laughter filled their home more days than most. Others looked at their relationship hoping to emulate what they had together.

But no matter how devoted Anna was to Samuel, her true love and forever groom would be Jesus. She met Jesus for the first time personally one Resurrection Sunday as a little girl. Anna was raised in a Christian home and attended church regularly, like many of her friends in her neighborhood. The Easter just before her ninth birthday was the service that changed Anna's life forever. Inwardly, while quietly sitting in her family's usual pew, she experienced the love of Jesus in such a real way that she would never be the same again. Despite her tender young age, there was no denying the very moment she believed. The confidence, the knowing, the assurance of Jesus' love was so present she felt one with love itself. *"God is love." 1 John 4:16*

Easter was no longer a story or a holiday to Anna. She knew, really knew that Jesus was an actual living person who demonstrated His love to all people by sacrificing Himself on a cross so that any person choosing to believe in Him would be forgiven of their sins and have eternal life with God. For the first time, she realized that Jesus' death for all people included her individually too. Tears rolled down her cheeks as the Truth set in deep within her heart. *"For God so loved the world that he gave his only begotten son, that whosoever believeth in him should not perish, but have everlasting life."* John 3:16

The revelation of God's love that filled Anna placed a hunger inside her to get to know Him in a new way. It felt to Anna as if life had begun again for her in that moment. Like she was actually born again in this world, but this time as a new person. Fresh start, do over, clean slate. *"...Verily, verily, I say unto thee, except a man be born again, he cannot see the kingdom of God." John 3:3*

Not long after that special Easter Sunday, on May 15, 1956 to be exact, Anna walked the aisle of the Hillsdale Community Church and professed out loud to her church family her belief in Jesus as her personal Lord and Savior. That very same evening, she was baptized in the church's baptismal pool making public her inner change. From that day forward, Jesus pursued her at every turn. *"...that he which hath begun a good work in you will perform it until the day of Jesus Christ." Philippians 1:6*

8

Monday morning, time for Rebecca to get serious. She started every week with the same attitude, a mixture of guilt from a wild weekend and determination to start fresh, and sober. Wondering how long she could keep up this pace, Rebecca slung her back pack over her left shoulder and headed out the door to Biology class.

Once seated in her classroom, she brought out her cell phone and scrolled through her day's schedule. She spotted "Sew What?" at 6pm. Homework in Calculus, a test in History on Wednesday, a paper due Friday in Literature. A hundred excuses began to run through her mind.

Then she remembered the overwhelming peace she experienced the first time she read the ad on the job posting board that day in the student center. The peace was stronger than her excuses. 6pm could not come sooner.

———————————

On Monday mornings, Emma headed to the Plaza Hotel downtown where she worked as a front desk clerk. Spending her days in the resort high rise provided a sort of escape from her woes. She enjoyed meeting and greeting all the travelers hoping some day to partake in similar pleasures.

Emma worked two jobs. Desk clerk by day, waitress by night. Her usual schedule was 8am-4:30pm at the Plaza Hotel, then 6pm-11pm at Necutt's Bar and Grill. She would drive through the bank teller almost daily en route to the restaurant to deposit her tip money from the previous night. Waitressing was supposed to be a job she left behind a decade ago. However, a looming divorce and little expectation of child support gave Emma good reason to wait tables in addition to her day job.

Realizing she would probably need to stop waitressing around her third trimester, she managed her money very carefully. She wanted to save all the money she could before the baby arrived in May. Her boss at Necutt's was a very nice man already approving her maternity leave plans. Being a sports pub, she figured she would work through basketball season which wrapped up in March.

Emma had requested the night off at the Necutt's in order to check out the "Sew What?" group. At the last minute, she second guessed her decision knowing the bills coming due. Monday Night Football brought in big tipping customers. She really could not afford a social life right now. Excuses poured into her mind, one after another.

Then she remembered the overwhelming joy she experienced the first time she read the ad on the customer service bulletin board in the Kroger. The joy was stronger than her excuses. She could hardly wait until 6pm.

Like any other morning, Bonnie left for work by 7:30am. Just being a Monday easily justified her to order a frozen caramel coffee with a whipped cream topping and slice of pound cake at the drive through on her way into the office.

At the next red light, she glanced down at her planner and saw that tonight began the "Sew What?" gathering. She began to dwell on the work load ahead of her. She desperately wanted to bail on her decision to go to the group that evening.

Bonnie could always count on her career when everything or everyone failed her. Without her job, she could not imagine what would become of her life. She could not chance that a social obligation might interfere with her work demands. Going to a non-work related activity felt like a defeat to her. Where is the productivity? Why be with other people? Bonnie's mind was becoming so full of excuses that she felt her chest tightening unable to breathe.

Then she remembered the overwhelming comfort she experienced the first time she read the ad in the Herald. The comfort was stronger than her excuses. She was ready for 6pm to arrive.

Monday mornings were Maggie's favorite. A new week, a new beginning. Matt was sure to find employment this week. Their break had to be right around the next corner.

When she met up with Matt at breakfast, she noticed that he was not his enthusiastic self. The job search, the shelter life, the debt were taking a toll on him badly. She wanted to share with him her excitement about the sewing class tonight. But after seeing Matt's face, she changed her mind about mentioning anything to him about it.

Maybe she should change her mind about going period? Her husband needed her. Her children needed her. Why go anyway? Even if she sewed curtains, where would she hang them? Excuses were all she could hear in her head. She struggled to fight back the tears welling up in her courageous eyes.

Then she remembered the overwhelming hope she experienced the first time she read the ad in the Chrysalis Center class brochure. The hope was stronger than her excuses. *Come 6pm, come.*

9

Anna reminisced while she rummaged through her old sewing room preparing for her first class. Her mind started racing ahead. How many students would her home accommodate? Where would she get the extra machines? Would they know how to sew or be just beginners?

Her thoughts continued to wander until she deliberately stopped herself, remembering to go to God FIRST before she planned any further. Anna knew from experience to pray about an idea in order to discern the Lord's directions from her own thoughts. *"A man's heart deviseth his way: but the Lord directeth his steps." Proverbs 16:9*

Anna wanted the direction of the group to please God so she desired Him to be the lesson planner. As she pondered different project possibilities, she would take them to prayer. She would pray until peace came about an idea. Pray and wait, then wait and pray. Surrendering her own agenda was often hard, but knowing how much her Father loved her, she knew His answer was best. *"Trust in the Lord with all thine heart; and lean not unto thine own understanding. In all thy ways acknowledge him, and he shall direct thy paths." Proverbs 3:5-6*

Not until Anna had peace in her heart about any matter did she take the next step. She had not always been so patient, but time had taught her waiting was a blessing, an accelerated season of growth.

Anna always loved when God would add confirmation to that peace in her heart, like her own special surprise. Though she learned not to rely on her emotions, those surprise confirmations made her feel so loved knowing God cared about even the smallest details of her life. *"But the very hairs of your head are all numbered."* Matthew 10:30

Sometimes an instruction would be spoken to Anna's heart and be confirmed by a scripture brought quickly to her mind. Other times God spoke to Anna through an open door, an opportunity that fulfilled a personal desire that she only confided in to God. Still other times, God's direction for her was confirmed by a timely word of wisdom offered from a mature friend in Christ. Anna could recognize God in her circumstances no matter how He chose to reveal Himself. *"My sheep hear my voice, and I know them, and they follow me:"* John 10:27

After spending time with the Lord and in His Word, her picture of the group was taking shape. Anna envisioned teaching a sewing lesson followed by a time of sharing conversation and sharing a new recipe. Perhaps dessert, along with some coffee or tea. Baking after all was her second favorite hobby!

She was so excited to see who the Lord would lead to the group. Anna rejoiced knowing full well this new adventure was God's plan. *"And there ye shall eat before the Lord your God, and ye shall rejoice in all that ye put your hand unto, ye and your households, wherein the Lord thy God hath blessed thee."*

Deuteronomy 12:7

10

Rebecca finished her last class at 4:30pm giving her just enough time to stop by her apartment for a quick bite. If not for prepackaged noodles, six for $1, her cabinets would probably go bare. She had become quite creative with this bargain meal. Sometimes, after boiling the wavy noodles, she would drain the broth and add peanut butter giving it a nutty flavor. Other times, she would prepare it as a soup and add ketchup giving it a tomato base. Either recipe hit the spot.

For a split second, Rebecca brainstormed about producing a "College Cookbook" as a way to help her cash crunch. Then again, she would not have a cash crunch if she cut back partying. A cash flow problem seemed much easier to face than a drinking problem. Besides, she was confident her lifestyle was just a phase. A stage that will be way behind her come graduation. And if not, no one was getting hurt.

Emma's day at the Plaza Hotel ended at the usual time of 4:30pm. Since her shift at Necutt's generally began at 6pm, tonight's sewing class would make no difference to her routine. She had grown accustomed to rushing from place to place in order to meet her hectic schedule.

Sitting in her car in the Plaza Hotel parking lot, Emma decided to pause a few moments before starting up the engine. She pulled out a small lunch cooler, unzipped the top, and pulled out an apple and banana. On the days she worked at Necutt's, she usually ate dinner there at the restaurant. A free meal was a benefit she really appreciated on her tight budget. Today she packed a snack knowing she would be heading straight to the sewing class.

As she sat in the quiet, peeling her banana, she began to blink long and slowly. Fighting back sleep, she wondered how long she could keep up this pace? How long she would be safe from Jake? Was this all there was to life now? Work, worry, work.

It was early for Bonnie to leave the office at 4:30pm. Her colleagues glanced up at her oddly as she passed by their cubicles. Her reputation was to be first in and last out so this sudden departure was cause for confusion. Ignoring their stares, she headed out of the building and into the parking garage toward her car.

The short walk to the car winded her, reminding Bonnie just how badly she needed to get in shape. Dieting was hard for Bonnie, but exercise was even harder. Bonnie was convinced she could not work out until after she dropped a few pounds. Excuse or truth, neither one was getting her any healthier.

Maggie was more than ready to venture out to the sewing club. She had a difficult day and her strength was fading fast. The longer commute to her job from the shelter was taking its toll on her. She regretted not going straight from her job to the class because she did not want Matt or the children to see her so weary.

She bumped into Matt in the entrance foyer where new people were being signed in as residents. After a quick visit with her hubby, Maggie made her way upstairs to freshen herself in the ladies bathroom closest to her quarters. For starters, she removed the elastic band from her ponytail and shook her wavy chestnut hair free. A little mouthwash, new deodorant and she would be back on her way again.

Maggie stopped to study her face in the mirror searching the image to see if she could find the little girl lost in this tired woman's face. She hoped her youthful spirit would return again one day. Before it was too late.

11

Rebecca was first to arrive, parking her dark blue Land Rover right in front of the address from the ad. The two story house was painted a bright white with hunter green shutters. The sidewalk leading up to the large front porch was lined with viburnum, waist high and full, a shrub hearty enough to survive almost any weather. Rebecca approached the house slowly, wanting to take in all the charm.

"Come on in," Anna invited with a wave of her arm. Anna smiled warmly as she watched Rebecca head up her porch stairs.

"Hi. I'm Rebecca," reaching up to shake hands from the bottom step.

Anna instead opened her arms wide, offering a welcome embrace. Rebecca dropped her arm to her side, climbed the few steps to the porch landing and hugged Anna as if she had known her all her life.

After they released one another, Anna introduced herself. "Hi Rebecca. I'm Anna. *So* nice to meet you. I am glad you came tonight."

Just then, Emma pulled up and turned off her engine. Taking a deep breath, she stepped out of the car and headed toward the house. Once she spotted the two ladies on the porch, she sensed she had the right place.

"Hello there," Anna announced, motioning her to come join in.

Stretching her arms outward now, Anna waited for Emma to reach the top of her porch stairs. There they hugged like long time friends.

Then Anna stepped back to greet her new guest. "My name is Anna and this is Rebecca," nodding toward where Rebecca stood.

"Hi. I'm Emma. Thanks for having me." Emma glanced around the porch, noticing a lovely swing hooked to the left of the front door. She could imagine gently swinging back and forth, sipping tea, and listening to nothing but crickets in the night air.

Bonnie arrived next, parking behind the line of cars forming in front of Anna's house. Before stepping out, she lowered the visor and checked her teeth in the mirror. She had just finished off a burger and fries, not knowing if there would be food served or not at the class. After a quick inspection of her smile, she closed her visor and opened her car door.

Coming straight from the office, Bonnie had on a black pin-stripped pant suit with a grey cotton blouse underneath that picked up the color of the stripe in her suit. As she stood up, she smoothed out her outfit with both hands and noticed a small grease stain on her blouse. She fumed inside, sure that it just happened from her fast food choice. Yanking her blazer closer together, she slammed the car door shut and marched ahead.

Bonnie continued toward the house, only looking up every few steps. She felt more comfortable watching her own feet move along rather than focusing on her destination.

"Good evening," Anna called out.

Bonnie looked up and climbed the front porch stairs, "Good evening."

Arms outstretched, Anna met Bonnie with a long hug. As Bonnie stayed in Anna's firm embrace, her anger subsided. Tears glistened in Bonnie's eyes as she realized how long it had been since she experienced human touch.

Anna brought her hands to the top of Bonnie's shoulders, "Hi. I am Anna. Welcome."

"I'm Bonnie. Nice to meet you."

"Let me introduce you to the others." Gesturing to each young lady, "Rebecca and Emma. This is Bonnie."

Bonnie returned their smiles, hoping they would see her as a potential friend. Girlfriends had hurt and disappointed her in the past, but she was open to try once more.

Maggie was the final student to show. Seeing a group of women gathered on the porch, she felt pressed to hurry, not wanting to be late. Quickly, she hopped out of her car and started for the house. She kept a fast pace, trying to ignore how fast her heart was racing inside her chest. Tension increased the closer she came to the front porch. She was so nervous that the other ladies would find out she was staying at the Chrysalis Center.

Then suddenly she locked eyes with Anna as she began climbing the stairs. Maggie's secret shame faded as Anna pulled her in close for a much needed hug.

Anna welcomed Maggie to the group and introduced the students one by one. They all gave her a warm and reassuring smile. Maggie gave a pleasant nod back in return. She knew instantly that she had found a home, if only for a night.

12

Anna opened her front door and slid inside with the ladies filing in behind her. After entering the foyer, Anna suggested they hang their purses and jackets on the coat rack to their immediate right. Next to the rack sat a long cherry wood storage trunk with a pair of white tennis shoes lined up along side. The trunk was covered with a cushioned seat upholstered in an autumn leaf cross stitch, both a practical and beautiful piece. The ladies hung up their coats and bags, then they slipped off their shoes as they saw Anna initiate.

The inviting entrance ushered in Anna's guests, making them feel right at home. Her place felt like a sanctuary, a secure and peaceful haven from the outside world.

"Please, make yourself at home," Anna urged. "Have a look see and then meet back here in the foyer to begin sewing time."

Wide-eyed, the ladies took Anna up on her offer to explore their surroundings. The interior was decorated in rich earth tones of harvest brown, khaki green, soft butter cream and crisp winter white. Most of the furniture looked to be precious antiques possibly handed down through several generations. It was obvious that Anna took good care of her home. Simple and uncluttered, yet a real personal feel in each room. Framed photographs of different sizes were displayed in a variety of unexpected places. Unique clusters were found on book shelves, table ends, dressers and even countertops. Some pictures in full color, others in black and white. Lots of loved ones spanning time. No serious or portrait style poses in sight; candid shots of laughter and joy were the only choices displayed.

Near the front window in the corner of the formal living room sat a black Wurlitzer piano. A music book was open and the ivory and black keys were exposed, suggesting this nook was a favorite spot in Anna's charming home.

After wandering a bit, they met back in the foyer as instructed. Next Anna led them to the sewing room where they would settle for the evening. There were two sewing machines in the room, a long table with two folding chairs, a sofa, end table, several lamps as well as a large overhead fluorescent light fixture. The room was cozy as well as functional.

Bookshelves lined the left hand wall from floor to ceiling. The top shelves were filled with numerous books in all different shapes, sizes and colors. The bottom shelves held clear containers or pretty baskets filled with a variety of sewing notions like pin cushions, threads and bobbins. Both convenience and comfort appeared to be the aim of the room's design.

"Take a seat, ladies, wherever you would like," Anna suggested while pointing out several available places to sit. "As you know, tonight is our first class and we will begin by discussing the objective of the course."

Anna continued, "The objective is for you to experience a love of sewing." She paused to make eye contact with each student before she went on, "With that passion, you will create beautiful works to enjoy and to share. The creations will inspire others to seek out the joy of sewing on their own."

Looking around the room, Anna studied the women's faces. She saw their eyes sparkle with excitement and curiosity. Smiles began to break out one by one. After observing that the ladies arrived scared and weary, Anna was delighted to witness new signs of hope in their expressions.

"Let's start by selecting your projects. What do you see yourself sewing? What purpose will your project have? Will it meet a need? Or will it simply bring joy? Will it be something to keep? Or something to give?"

Anna explained, "The assignment this week is to search your heart and search your surroundings. Your project lies where your heart and surroundings meet. Bring your vision to the group and be prepared for an adventure."

By the night's end, the women began to appear refreshed and renewed. Anna hugged each one individually as they slowly left her home for the evening.

13

After sewing class, Rebecca had planned to drop by First Stop to catch up with her buddies. She drove by and saw students coming and going, laughing and stumbling along the sidewalk by the night club. Her plan was to drive home and then walk back to the bar so she could drink without the worry of driving.

Upon arrival at her apartment building, she circled the parking lot looking for an open spot. For a moment, she contemplated staying in, curling up on the couch, and watching TV. She had a flash back of her high school years when she and her sister would share a bowl of popcorn while enjoying their favorite sitcoms. Rebecca missed those days, so innocent and joyful. Attending the sewing class gave her a glimpse of that feeling again. She felt a quiet contentment during her visit at Anna's house that she had not experienced in a very long time.

She parked her car close to her front door, turned off the engine, and sat wrestling with her decision. Stay or go. Just then a chirp sound came from inside her purse. She reached in and fished out her cell phone recognizing the sound of an incoming text.

"Where are you?" read the text from her friend Janie.

Rebecca shoved her car keys in her purse as she thought how to answer. "I'm on my way," she replied at last.

As soon as Rebecca pushed the send button, she felt an urgency to hurry and meet up with her group. Deep down though, she realized her need to hurry was more closely linked to her need to drink a large cold draft beer. It was 9pm, far past the hour she typically started to indulge. Once she was mingling and drinking, all would feel right again.

I will stay in another night, Rebecca reasoned. *There's always tomorrow night.*

It was rare for Emma to be home by 9pm. She usually did not get in until after 11pm once all her tables were cleared and her section was closed. Some waitresses at Necutt's stay as late as 2am or 3am, but Emma has only worked those shifts occasionally, and only when she had the following day off from her hotel job. Grateful to be home early, Emma decided to take a bath then jump into bed with several books she picked up from the library.

Emma's stack included parenting, pregnancy and relationship titles. All topics she hoped would help her sort through her situation. Staying busy hid her pain for the most part. But as soon as she slowed down, there it was as real as anything. A deep ache in her gut. A hurt beyond explanation. How would she ever reconcile the picture of marriage she had from her youth with the reality of today?

Nestled under the covers, Emma turned her bedside lamp on and plopped the pile of books on her lap. She was ready to find an answer, a fix for her sadness. As she opened the first book, Emma stopped for a minute to reflect back on the evening. Even after just one night, she sensed a feeling of belonging at the sewing class. Anna made her feel accepted, genuinely accepted. Not pretend, but for real.

If only I was worthy of love, Emma cried. *Too many mistakes, too big to forget.*

Bonnie rushed into her apartment almost slamming the door behind her. She pressed her back up against the door as if holding someone dangerous out. Finally, she exhaled as tears welled up in her eyes. *I will not go back, I can not go back,* Bonnie vowed. She knew she let her guard down tonight at the sewing class. Not in an obvious outward way, but inside she caved. She liked them and even thought they liked her too. Soft is risky, too risky. If she were to go back, it would have to be different. Afraid of disappointment, Bonnie knew she would have to keep a big distance between herself and the women, especially Anna.

Amazing Anna, so kind and gentle. When Anna embraced her as they greeted, Bonnie felt as if she was in her own mother's arms. The actual, physical arms of her mother. Same grip, same warmth. The memory was strong and surreal.

51

Losing her mother at twelve years old brought an indescribable grief to Bonnie's life. Her source of strength, guidance, and unconditional love vanished. Mama was her anchor without whom Bonnie became adrift. After her mama's passing, Bonnie all but shut down. Rather than reaching out for others, she pushed them away. Instead she turned to work and food, exactly where she hides now twenty years later.

Shaking her head to shift the memory from her mind, she darted toward the kitchen. She opened the cabinet to the right of the stove and stared at the contents. After a few seconds, she shut the cabinet, turned and crossed the room. Next she opened the refrigerator and resumed staring. Then she shut the refrigerator door and opened the freezer door wide. At last, she made her choice. Ice cream.

Pulling out the tub, she grabbed a large spoon and her favorite bowl. She began dishing out the chocolate chunk dessert, scoop after scoop. With her emotions starting to ease, she put away the tub and made her way to the living room.

Why did Mama have to die? Why? Bonnie agonized. *Why?*

Maggie intentionally chose the longest route back to the Chrysalis Center. She drove under the speed limit attempting to further prolong the trip. Her curfew was not until 10pm which gave her over an hour to get back. She truly wanted to savor this evening.

The car provided her alone time, something she desperately needed in order to process all her family had been through over the last few months. As a matter of fact, this was the first time she had been alone since their move to the shelter. Indeed, this time was special.

Maggie didn't want to leave Anna's home. She almost *couldn't* leave. There was what could best be described as a 'tugging' on Maggie's heart to stay. The tug was not one of restraint, but of security, protection and rest. All her cares seemed to not even exist while she was at the class tonight. A respite Maggie craved greatly.

Anna was such a delight to be around, so pleasant and sweet. As odd as it sounds, her very presence seemed to give off what she could only describe as an aroma of some kind. *What was that?* Maggie questioned. She wondered if the smell was just her imagination, or was it real.

Maggie continued to search her memory bank. She couldn't recall the scent, so distinct and unusual. It was very different from a designer, store bought perfume. *What was that fragrance?*

LOVE. Strangely enough, the only word that came to her mind was *love*. There was no other possible description. She sat puzzled, yet convinced of her conclusion. Maggie drew in a deep breath followed by a long exhale. *Mmmm, love.* Yes, if love indeed emanated a fragrance, it was surely Anna's signature scent!

However brief, Maggie was grateful for the evening and the opportunity to recharge. Spotting the parking lot in the distance, Maggie was suddenly jolted from her reverie. The time had come to snap to it, put on the mask, and gear up for her return to the center, to her real life.

Maggie was committed to being there for her husband and children even if she was collapsing from the inside out. She would not let her fear show, not even a hint.

How can I stay strong? Maggie desired. *From where will I get the strength?*

Anna lingered on her front porch watching the tail lights fade in the distance. She kept her gaze long after the cars drove out of sight. Lifting her left hand, she placed her fingertips across her lips and drew in a deep breath through her nose. She closed her eyes and exhaled slowly as she pictured each of her students one by one.

Rebecca, Emma, Bonnie and Maggie.

Anna clasped both of her hands together and turned her face to the night sky. Her voice rose just above a whisper, *"Come to me, all you who are weary and burdened, and I will give you rest." Matthew 11:28*

14

Rebecca could hardly wait until the weekend. The week days seemed to drag on while the weekends just flew right by. Coping with the demands of her lifestyle was exhausting. She realized these consequences were self-imposed, yet she stayed the course, the party course.

Though Rebecca deemed class attendance optional, her professors were not of the same opinion. Each course at the University had a participation component derived primarily of each student's attendance record. This mark was undoubtedly Rebecca's lowest grade in every class she had this semester.

To Rebecca, skipping classes was essential to college life. She would skip one class to catch up on sleep, skip another class to do homework and skip yet another class to study. If she had an exam in a class, she would show up for sure. Other than that, she chose homework, study or sleep. With getting in almost every night past 2am, sleep was the most popular of her choices. Convinced this juggling act was the only way to fit it all in, Rebecca rolled over in her bed pulling the covers with her. A little more sleep, and she would be good to go.

Besides, this snoozing time was still productive she reasoned. She could plan her sewing project while she dozed in and out of her early morning slumber. What would she make? A jacket. No, too complex. A skirt. No, wouldn't wear it enough. A blanket. No, plenty of those. How about a purse or hand bag? Yes, that's it. A girl can never have too many accessories!

––––––––––––––––

Wednesdays and Thursdays were typically Emma's scheduled days off at the hotel *and* the restaurant. This set schedule was the key to Emma keeping up her pace. Having the two days off together from both jobs gave her body the chance to rest and recharge. She was so grateful that each of her bosses agreed to that request early on in her pregnancy. Emma was also thrilled when Paul, her Necutt's boss, permitted her Monday nights off as well to take her sewing class.

More important than reviving physically, Emma needed that time every week to revive emotionally. She was constantly battling discouragement over her past choices and fear about the future. Five months pregnant now. Too late to turn back. Too late to undo her mistakes. Mistakes. Mistakes?

Marrying Jake, knowing his capacity for losing control, was definitely a mistake. Emma just wanted love and marriage so badly. She had been blinded to Jake's dark side by the fairytale ending that played in her mind. Yet, the cost was too high and too dangerous to stay with him. No, leaving Jake was *not* a mistake.

But Emma could never call her baby a mistake. Her friends thought so though. Her best friend, Kate, even asked her if she was going to keep it. *It!* How could Kate call her baby or any baby for that matter an "it"? Well, despite her critics, Emma loved the baby growing inside her and vowed to make a good life for the both of them. To shake off any doubt, Emma purposely envisioned taking her baby on a stroll through Carillion Park. It is a sunny day, slight breeze, birds singing.

Having the day off, she decided to go to the fabric store near the Parkway mall to browse for ideas for her sewing project. Emma was really looking forward to her next class after having such a tremendous time on Monday.

A crib blanket came to her imagination. She pictured a beautiful design of lambs running in a soft green meadow under a bright blue sky with puffy white clouds. Nearing the store now, she could hardly wait to begin her search among the rolls of material. Oh, how she hoped to find her dream print.

Bonnie shook her head in disgust and stormed into her office slamming the door behind her. She pulled out her desk chair, sat down and began to type out an email to her assistant recounting the conversation that just took place between them. Contempt, anger and loathing were all the emotions that came to her mind as she pounded steadily on her keyboard. She would also need to copy the email to the owners of the firm knowing full well they would never question her decision.

Another assistant fired, her third one this year. The reason was the same for every termination, insubordination. Bonnie was convinced she was not a difficult boss, but that she merely had difficult employees. With jaws clenched, she clicked the send button and there went another person from her life.

Bonnie prided herself on being the last one to leave the office each night. Although she hoped her colleagues saw this practice as dedication, she knew that it was not just loyalty that kept her late, but loneliness. Despite this afternoon's turmoil, Bonnie remained at work well past 7:30pm. Finally, anger gave way to fatigue and she decided to head home.

As Bonnie opened her front door, she heard her telephone ringing. Hastily, she removed her keys from the lock and hurried toward the phone. Her heart leaped with anticipation as personal calls were so rare these days.

"Hello," Bonnie said.

"Is Bill there?" the voice on the other end inquired.

"You must have the wrong number," she replied and slowly placed the receiver in the cradle.

Bonnie slid off her loafers, shuffled to her bedroom and laid face down on her bed. Then she turned on her side, and curled her legs up to her chest while tucking her head down into the fetal position. She reached behind herself for a pillow and pulled it in hard to her stomach. After wallowing a bit, she stretched down to the foot of her bed for her comforter and yanked it up over her shoulders and under her chin.

There was so much pain that needed to be released from her soul, but when Bonnie opened her mouth to cry, not a single sound could be heard. It had been so long since she let go. Finally, one tear rolled from her eye. That one tear led to another until she was sobbing, almost uncontrollably. Minutes seemed to turn into hours and soon Bonnie drifted off to sleep.

When Bonnie awoke the next morning, she was relieved that her first thoughts were of her sewing class and of her assignment to pick a project. Noticing how relaxed she felt made her realize her project was right there, wrapped around her body. A comforter. Yes, a comforter. A new comforter was definitely in order.

Friday evenings were especially hard for the Tucker family. Actually Friday nights were hard for most residents at the Chrysalis Center for the Homeless. While a few families would move out each weekend, even more seemed to be moving in. The crowded conditions and lack of privacy were wearing on Matt and Maggie's marriage. Yes, shelter life was definitely taking its toll on their once happy union.

Before Matt lost his job, the couple looked forward to their weekends together. They would spend their time simply relaxing, playing with their children or working on a project around their home. Now, weekends meant fretting and worrying about how and when they would be able to move into a place of their own again. Their plan was to rent a house or an apartment in their children's current school district. Limiting any more big changes for their children was very important to both Maggie and Matt. They had been through enough.

At the very minimum, they would need to save enough money for a security deposit and first month's rent. Although Matt had several promising job interviews, he had yet to find sustainable employment. Maggie continued to work at Macon Paper Company with her paycheck covering the car payment and auto insurance. Many residents at the center relied on public transportation so the Tuckers counted themselves fortunate to have a car, even though they had to share. They had sold their second car awhile back while trying to reorganize and save their home.

Tonight they sat face to face in the common dining hall with a school lunch room style cafeteria table between them. Abigail, now seven years old, sat right up next to Maggie while her brother Andrew, almost ten, drew close beside Matt. Without a word, the four picked at their meal of beef stroganoff, a regular dish served more likely for how far it would stretch than for its taste.

Maggie broke the silence, "I have to select a project for my sewing class this Monday."

No one answered. Determined to lift the mood, she continued, "What do you think of linen placemats and matching napkins?"

Still no response. Maggie pressed on, "We could set the table in our new home with them. What do you think?"

Matt realized how hard Maggie was trying to cheer everyone up. "New placemats and napkins will be perfect, especially because they will be made by you."

Maggie and Matt exchanged smiles and a warm glance. Abigail and Andrew joined in as tentative smiles spread across their faces.

The mere thought of her sewing class brought hope to Maggie's heart. And tonight, her hope lightened the hearts of those she held most dear. Whatever special feeling she received from Anna and the sewing class, she was delighted to be a partaker and to pass a little of that feeling on to her family, even if just a little.

Anna cherished her early morning quiet time with the Lord. At 6am, with a hot cup of coffee in her hand, she headed to her favorite chair in the den. After turning on the lamp, she sat down, took hold of her Bible from the end table, and pulled a soft blanket off the back of her chair to lie on her lap. *"O God, thou art my God; early will I seek thee: my soul thirsteth for thee...." Psalms 63:1* Today, Anna read chapter forty six from the book of Psalms knowing she would find comfort and encouragement. She reread the chapter several times meditating on the words as she allowed the scriptures to take root in her heart. *"God is our refuge and strength, a very present help in trouble...." Psalms 46:1 "Be still, and know that I am God:......." Psalm 46:10*

Anna slowly closed her Bible resting her hands on top and prayed aloud just above a whisper. *"Father God, I love you and I love this time with you. In your presence, I find such great joy. You are an awesome God. I praise you for all you have done and all you are going to do in me and through me. Forgive me for ever doubting your promises. You are a faithful Father. Create in me a clean heart, O God; and renew a right spirit within me. (Psalm 51:10) Thank you for your mercy, grace and love. Thank you for revealing your purpose for this season. Thank you that I will still bear fruit in my old age. (Psalms 92:14) Father, I know the desire to form the sewing class came from you. Thank you for bringing these beautiful women into my life. O, how I could see pain in their eyes. Even in their laughter, I could see the sorrow of their hearts. (Proverbs 14:13) Equip me to minister to them, Lord. Rebecca, Emma, Bonnie and Maggie. I pray you touch each one right now, Father. Heal their broken hearts and bind up their wounds. (Psalms 147:3) Give them beauty for ashes, the oil of joy for mourning, and the garment of praise for the spirit of heaviness. (Isaiah 61:3) In Jesus' name, Amen."*

15

Monday rolled around fast, Rebecca realized, as she slowly turned on to Albert Street. She so looked forward to sharing her project idea with the sewing group tonight. While approaching the front stairs to Anna's home, Rebecca spotted her teacher sitting quietly on the porch swing. Anna rose once she caught eyes with her first student of the evening. Wearing a mid-length periwinkle blue dress, Anna looked beautiful with her long thick hair pulled back in a single braid that draped down the middle of her back. Her once blonde color now shimmered with what seemed to be white sparkles throughout her hair. At 64 years old, Anna was still a natural beauty. She smiled, "Welcome back, Rebecca. Good to see you."

Before long, they were joined by Emma, Bonnie and Maggie. The five women hugged as if old friends, then made their way inside. The sewing room looked different this week. Instead of the chairs being under the various tables, they were positioned in a circle and centered in the room. The setting was very intimate with only table lamps for lighting and soft music in the background. Anna took a seat first and the ladies instinctively followed her example.

Anna began, "Your assignment this week was to select your sewing project for our class. I am sure you came up with some wonderful ideas. Who would like to be the first to share?"

"I would," announced Emma. "Well, my baby is due in May and I would like to sew a blanket for the crib." Reaching down into a bag next to her chair, Emma pulled out a quilted material in soft pastel colors. She opened the fabric up lengthwise so the pattern could be easily seen by the group. Holding it up just below her chin, she turned her body toward each woman as they nodded back their approval. Emma was once again pleased with her selection. A baby's delight, she thought, looking down at the white lambs running playfully on a green meadow under a bright blue sky. A baby's delight.

Anna sat on Emma's immediate left asked, "May I please hold your material and look at it up close?"

"Sure," Emma replied handing her the fabric.

The women gazed intently at Anna as she caressed the material between her fingers. They were excited to hear her comments on Emma's choice. Anna held the fabric up high above her shoulders with both hands as her eyes moved from left to right scanning the scenic pasture print. Then she laid the material down slowly on her lap. With her right hand, she ran her fingertips across one of the lambs as if petting an animal she knew in real life. Anna did not yet speak a word. Neither did the ladies. Rather, the class sat silently as they watched Anna study the design.

Anna closed her eyes and began to hum a sweet tune, all the while keeping her fingers resting on the lamb. Ever slightly, she rocked her head from side to side in time to her song. Anna seemed to be experiencing immense joy in that moment, almost as if visiting another time or place in her imagination.

Curious, Maggie interrupted her private thoughts, "Anna, I hope you do not mind me asking, but did you live on a farm before?"

"No. I have not lived on a farm," Anna claimed.

"You look so happy admiring the beautiful scenery on Emma's fabric. I would have thought for sure you must have lived on a farm at one time?" Maggie still doubted.

"No, I have not lived on a farm, but I *do* know a shepherd."

"By the look in your eyes, you must have cared for him very much," Rebecca commented, secretly hoping to duplicate that look in her own eyes one day. "Did you love him?"

"I still do," Anna professed.

With puzzled expressions on their faces, the ladies remained quiet as they made inquisitive glances at each other. None of the women dared a follow up question and Anna did not offer an explanation. At last, Bonnie spoke up, "May I go next?"

"Yes, Bonnie, we would love to hear about your project idea," Anna confirmed.

Bonnie grabbed the shopping bag next to her and brought it up on her lap. She could hardly believe she was here in this room, with these ladies, nonetheless participating full on. Though unlike her corporate persona, this moment felt so good to her, so authentic.

Pausing to take a deep breath, Bonnie pulled out a stack of folded material that looked like flannel at a distance. "I was thinking of a comforter for my bed," Bonnie described. "Soft, and warm, for winter."

Anna reached out towards Bonnie hinting for her to place the fabric in her hands. Bonnie carefully passed Anna the pile allowing her to examine the material just like she had done with Emma.

Lifting the bundle, Anna held it to the side of her cheek and tilted her head as if sleeping on a soft pillow. Once again, she seemed to drift into her own world. After a bit, Anna gave her approval.

"Excellent choice," Anna commended. "Comfort and rest is a need we all deeply share."

Reassured by Anna's words, Bonnie retrieved her flannel and returned it to her bag placing it back on the floor next to her chair. "A need I have for sure," Bonnie admitted, surprising herself by sharing.

Anna declared, "There is but one true way to find comfort and rest. The only true -----."

BANG, BANG, BANG!

16

Suddenly there was a loud banging from the other room, the noise cutting Anna off in mid-sentence. The ladies' eyes widened then darted back and forth at each other as they focused on listening closely.

"BANG, BANG, BANG!" There it was again.

This time Anna rose, smoothed the back of her dress, and rushed to the door to see who was there. She stood tip toed and peaked out the palladium glass window that made up the top part of her otherwise solid wood door.

Wary of the interruption, the women leaned forward in their seats straining to see what was happening. They watched the visit unfold from behind and concluded Anna must have known the person to have opened the door so freely.

From where the students sat, they could see Anna accept what looked like a cardboard box about the size of a microwave oven. She took a few steps to the side and set the box on the chest next to the front door. Though the exact words exchanged could not be heard, the high pitch in Anna's voice gave away her excitement. She nodded her head enthusiastically and then stretched forward for a quick hug. Full of energy, she turned, shut the door and practically skipped back to her seat in the circle.

As if nothing had just happened, Anna called out, "Maggie, it is your turn."

"Actually, I was hoping to go next week if that was alright with you?" Maggie begged, knowing she came empty handed. To her disappointment, there was not any fabric left when she shopped at the Chrysalis Store earlier today. And with only "Homeward Bound" bucks to spare, shopping elsewhere was out of the question.

Anna repeated, "Maggie, you have all you need. It is your turn."

"But, I--- " Maggie hesitated.

Anna nodded for her to begin.

"I want to make placemats for my family's dining room table." Maggie struggled to finish, fighting back tears. "I - I do not have material."

Anna stood and walked back to the bench where the cardboard box was placed. She returned to the sewing room and handed the delivery to Maggie. "Yes, you do."

Tears of joy formed in Maggie's eyes as she opened the box and realized what was inside. "Is this material really for me? Who – Who was that?" Maggie stammered overcome with emotion.

"Your family will sit before a marvelous feast, in your own home, at your own table, decorated with your own hand sewn, beautiful table linen," Anna pronounced confidently.

Wiping the tears off her face, Maggie wrapped both arms over top of the box as she worked on gaining her composure. As she embraced her mysterious gift, she turned and mouthed the words "thank you" to Anna.

With all eyes on their teacher, Anna clarified, "Maggie, *I* am not the one to thank. Neither was the stranger at the door." She continued, "This was a gift that met a *material* need in your life. Yet, there is still a better gift available, free and perfect. It is sufficient enough to meet *every* need in your life."

Abruptly, as if Rebecca was oblivious to the ongoing conversation, she blurted out, "May I go over my project now?" Her tone sounded hurried, even down right annoyed. The other students shot her back stern glares hoping to tame her impulsiveness. Not noticing the disharmony, Rebecca persisted, "May I go now?"

"Of course," Anna steadied her. "Please share with us, Rebecca. We are looking forward to hearing your idea."

Following Anna's lead, the rest of the ladies relaxed and prepared to listen to Rebecca's presentation. The tension eased, the mood restored. Just like that. Anna had a way about her that could soothe a soul.

"I would like to sew a bag. I mean a purse, like a tote. Uh, like a designer sack, sort of," Rebecca described in her youthful manner. "What do you think?"

Silence.

"I like it," Emma encouraged.

"So do I," agreed Maggie.

"Me too," Bonnie chimed in.

"All I know is that I have so much to carry. Too much. Way too much," Rebecca exclaimed. "I don't have anything big enough or strong enough to carry it all in."

"Well, I *love* it!" Anna cried out. "A bag is a wonderful idea." She smiled and clapped her hands together applauding the project. "Actually, Rebecca, there is a way you do not *have* to carry so much around."

Rebecca laughed. "You don't know my professors!"

All at once, the whole room was filled with laughter. Anna was especially happy seeing the ladies enjoy themselves and each other. The laughter continued while giggles brought on more giggles. Joy was long over due. And more fun than a good cry.

The laughter lingered as the women slowly made their way to the front door. Anna escorted them out on the front porch where they hugged and bid good bye for the evening. Until next time.

17

Where am I? Rebecca awoke asking herself. Unfamiliar with her surroundings, she scanned the strange room trying to piece together the night before. Her heart sank. *What have I done?* She looked over to the right and found her lab partner, Phil, snoring away. *What?* Dizzy and nauseas, she didn't think she could move. But she had to. She had to get out of there before Phil woke up.

How could this have happened? She was so angry with herself, but there was no time to stew. Rebecca carefully climbed out of the foreign bed and picked her clothes up off the floor. Dressing quickly, she tip toed toward the bedroom door. Phil moaned and stirred under the sheets. Rebecca turned the door knob so quietly hoping not to wake Phil any further. Another stir. Then she heard in a low garbled voice, "Bye Mel. I'll call you." She could barely make out his words. Except for *Mel.* She heard that word, crystal clear.

"Plaza Hotel. This is Emma. How may I help you?"

Emma recited her usual greeting when assigned the switchboard, jazzing it up on holidays now and again. "Happy Holidays", "Seasons Greetings", or anything else politically correct.

"Why didn't you take Stewart Street this morning? Why did you take the interstate?" the caller questioned.

Her stomach cramped. She could not breathe. *Jake.*

"Why put our baby at risk driving the highway?" Jake hollered.

She knew better than to answer him. Desperate to escape, Emma jumped up from her chair thinking of a way to flee the situation.

"Since when do you wear red? Whose attention are you trying to get? No one looked at you before you were pregnant, what makes you think they would look at you now?" Jake went on badgering.

Unable to speak, Emma clicked the disconnect button of the switchboard. She stood there numb and held onto her desk to keep from collapsing.

Multiple lines began ringing. Lights lit up across the board. Emma stepped out of the operator room and into the front desk area. She tugged at her coworker's arm motioning her to take over her duty for a minute.

Seeing Emma's panic, Brenda rushed to the phone room and positioned the head set. "Plaza Hotel. This is Brenda. How may I help you?"

"One moment. I'll connect you," Brenda said then quickly pushed several buttons to transfer the call.

"Plaza Hotel. This is ----."

Emma could hear the familiar screaming through the earpiece. *Jake.* Immediately, Brenda hung up the phone and proceeded to take the next call. Shaken and scared, Emma paced the floor not knowing what to do. As soon as there was a break between callers, Brenda walked over to Emma and demanded, "What is going on?"

"911, what is your emergency?"

"Yes. I think my employee is having a heart attack. Come quick," Mr. Hanson relayed barely able to catch his own breath under the circumstances.

"We are on our way. Please verify your address."

"256 North Main. Downtown. The Wright Tower, 12th floor. Hanson, Bradford, and Skeen. Hurry!"

"Yes, sir. Stay on the line."

Bonnie could hear the voices. She knew she was in trouble. Her eyelids were heavy. She was fighting consciousness. There was pressure and sharp pain with every breath.

"Bonnie. *Bonnie?* Can you hear me?" Mr. Hanson urged gently shaking her where she laid on the floor.

She tried her best to answer. No words would come. She wanted to tell them she was ok, that she was alive.

Or am I? Bonnie wondered. *Am I still alive?*

"Bonnie. *BONNIE?*"

"Ten days. I am sorry, Mr. and Mrs. Tucker. There are only ten days left in your stay here at the Chrysalis Center."

Maggie and Matt sat shocked in the admissions office as they listened to the director, Pam, explain their policies.

"There just aren't enough beds in town. Sixty days is the maximum length allowed," Pam instructed.

After absorbing the news, Matt stood up and looked Pam square in the eyes. He boldly agreed, "Yes ma'am. Ten days." Maggie then followed him out of the office and through the front door of the shelter. Matt walked one step ahead of Maggie stopping to sit at a bench across from the parking lot.

Matt dropped his face into his hands and hunched over his knees. Maggie sat down next to him and placed her hand on his shoulder in hopes of comforting her husband. Just as she began rubbing his back, she felt his body heave as his cry turned into a stifled, but desperate sob.

Matt, my sweet Matt.

Today was unseasonably warm for February. 68 degrees. Though spring was still many months away, Anna took this opportunity to give some TLC to her backyard garden. Not only did she want to get out and enjoy some sunshine, she also thought this mid-winter nurturing would produce a more bountiful crop come summer.

Her yard was considerably large for the neighborhood, almost a half an acre. The garden itself was approximately 20' x 9' and was positioned in the back right corner of the lot. She started out her day's project by raking off the dead leaves, putting them in trash bags and taking them to the curb. Next, she took a shovel and turned the dirt over, loosing it up, row by row. Then, she walked up and down the rows, spreading fertilizer on the freshly exposed soil. At last, just before sunset, Anna stood back and took a long look at all she had accomplished. She was grateful to the Lord for such a special day, a glimpse at her favorite season just around the corner.

Anna so looked forward to spring. She loved when the flowers would bloom and the green landscape would take the place of the wintery gray. The change of seasons fascinated her. She loved how creation mirrored life. Death and new birth. Seed time and harvest.

Gardening was more than a hobby to Anna. It was a marvelous, tangible way God demonstrated His promise of sowing and reaping. This summer, Anna desired a plentiful garden with more than enough to share with her sewing class. Tomatoes, lettuce, carrots. Onions, beans, cabbage.

"...*feed my sheep,*" the Holy Spirit brought John 21:16 to her remembrance.

"Yes, Lord," she answered out loud. "I will feed your sheep."

18

The day Rebecca dreaded had come. Wednesday. Biology lab. She contemplated skipping the class this Wednesday or even dropping it all together. With the semester coming to an end soon, she knew she should just hang in there and finish. She had come this far. Besides, facing Phil was inevitable. *What would she say? What would he say? He never called,* Rebecca thought. "Oh, that's right. He said he would call *Melanie!*" she murmured sarcastically underneath her breath.

The bell rang and Rebecca rushed to take her seat next to Phil. Texting mindlessly, Phil didn't look up or even seem to notice her sit down on her stool. The students noisily brought out their books, notebooks and pens as Mrs. Crausen began her phylum lecture.

While rummaging through her backpack, Rebecca and Phil caught eyes. A knot grew in Rebecca's stomach. *He didn't say anything!* Rebecca fumed. Zilch. Nada. Zip. *What did she expect anyway?* She chastised herself.

Rebecca tried her hardest to focus on the lesson at hand, but her thoughts kept drowning out her teacher's words. Before the ending bell even rung, Rebecca had already packed up her things ready to sprint out of the classroom. The less time together, the less communication she would have to analyze, then reanalyze and, of course, analyze again. She could not wait to get home and hide.

Unlocking her apartment door, she headed straight to the kitchen dropping her book bag on the floor next to the dining room table. She looked at the clock. 2:20pm. Happy hour didn't start at Alex's for another hour and forty minutes. A jump start on the "happy" sounded good to Rebecca. Relieved that she brought home a six pack from Tom's Tavern last night, Rebecca reached into her fridge and pulled out a cold one. Just the crack of the can brought a sense of calm to her being. She was tired of worrying about Phil, tired of worrying, period. *"Aahh!"* she sighed out loud taking extra large gulps of her favorite beer. *Quenched again. My dependable friend.*

Emma looked more in her rear view mirror than at the road while driving to Necutt's that afternoon. Her boss called earlier and asked her to work this evening, although she typically had Wednesdays scheduled off. She agreed to come in thinking she would feel safer at Necutt's than in her apartment alone. Her peace and security now shattered by yesterday's phone call to the hotel. She couldn't believe Jake followed her, or hired someone to follow her. *Who am I kidding? I certainly could believe it, typical Jake procedure.*

Emma had not wanted to tell her co-workers the details of her personal situation, but she felt she owed Brenda some explanation for coming to her rescue earlier. "Marriage problems," Emma simplified. "My husband is just a bit overwhelmed with the baby coming, that's all."

Brenda did not buy into Emma's story. Having heard Jake's ranting firsthand, she concluded that he had more than baby jitters. She decided not to pressure Emma with further questions, but reassured her that she was there for her as a friend.

It had been so long since Emma had confided in someone. She had always been too frightened or ashamed to share. Some episodes she figured were too hard to believe so she kept her life a secret. A sad secret that ate away at her soul little by little every day. Condemning herself had become second nature to her. But she was learning that dwelling on the past only delayed her dealing with the present. Something she could not afford to do, especially now.

She had run from Jake before, but this time was different. It was not just her life at stake any longer. Her baby needed her protection. The sound of Jake's voice resonated in her head. Just as she arrived at Necutt's, a chill of danger ran through her body like ice. Emma looked over her shoulder several times as she crossed the parking lot. *Will I ever be free? Truly free?*

Bonnie struggled to open her eyes. *Where am I?* She wondered. She blinked repeatedly to bring her vision into focus. As soon as she could make out her surroundings, the missing pieces of her memory started to come back together. She recognized the room to be in a hospital, cold and sterile. *How did I end up here?* She continued to question.

She looked out the window hoping to find a landmark that would identify which hospital. But Bonnie could see nothing except a flat roof top with numerous air conditioning units.

"I have to get out of here," she complained. Tearing back her covers, she attempted to get up until she realized she was hooked up to all sorts of medical equipment. Feeling pinned down and trapped, she began to search frantically for a nurse call button. Before she could locate it, help had arrived.

Nurse Kelly entered the room. With clipboard in hand, she smiled, "Good morning, Bonnie. I am here to check your vitals. How are you feeling today?"

"When did I get here?" Bonnie barked. "And what day is it?"

"You came in yesterday. Today is Wednesday, March 18th." Nurse Kelly explained politely.

Bonnie drew her eyebrows together and crunched up her forehead, "When can I go home?"

"Tomorrow......maybe," she replied picking up Bonnie's wrist to take her pulse. "You need to rest right now."

Bonnie chuckled, "Maybe? No, maybe. I will be leaving tomorrow. Do you understand?"

Nurse Kelly bit her lower lip not wanting to snap back at her patient's demeaning remark.

"It will depend on the results of your tests. They will be back by tomorrow morning."

With nothing left to say, Bonnie gave up the argument and rolled onto her side. *If only I had listened sooner. Much sooner.*

———————————

On Wednesday morning, Maggie and Matt, met downstairs for breakfast like usual. Their children had already left for school. They had to come up with a plan. "After paying this month's car payment and insurance, we have $870 left," reported Maggie.

"That won't be enough to rent a place. We need twice that to cover a deposit and the first month," Matt pointed out.

"I don't get paid again until Friday, April 4th. Our ten days will be up before then," Maggie fretted.

"I have an interview at 2pm today," Matt offered though inside he knew it was too late. They were ten days from living on the streets. His heart crushed feeling like he let his family down.

"You better get ready then," Maggie said mustering up all the courage she had not to cry.

"I better," Matt agreed.

They walked out of the dining hall together arm and arm. The couple stopped in the foyer before heading to their separate living quarters for morning showers. Matt turned toward Maggie taking her face in his hands. He kissed her softly and stroked her

81

hair off her forehead. Looking deeply into her eyes, he said, "Listen, Maggie, I want you to go see the director today about you and the children transferring to a women's shelter."

"Matt, NO. I won't leave you. We are in this together," Maggie stood firm.

"Yes, Maggie. You must," he explained. "I'll be fine. We will be together again soon. Once I find a job and have enough money for a place of our own," Matt promised.

Maggie couldn't believe what she was hearing. She pulled from his embrace and ran to her room on the second floor. Out of breath, she sat down on the hard floor and rested the back of her head against her bunk. Their conversation whirled in her mind. She was heartsick by the very idea of separating. Maggie loved Matt so much. *This can't be happening. It can't be.*

Anna's phone rang. "Hello," she answered.

"Hello, Anna?" Bonnie confirmed.

"Yes," Anna replied.

"This is Bonnie from sewing class. I remembered you gave us your phone number the first night we met. I am sorry to bother you," Bonnie started with a catch in her voice.

"No bother at all, Bonnie. I am here for you. What's going on?" Anna sensed something was wrong.

"I am in the hospital. They *said* I had a heart attack," Bonnie explained denying the seriousness of her condition.

"What hospital are you in?" Anna probed while grabbing her purse off her kitchen counter.

"Dayton General," Bonnie was quick to answer.

"I will be there in thirty minutes," Anna assured her and hung up the phone.

Anna sat down momentarily at her kitchen table and pulled out a small Bible from her purse. She yearned to read a bit for strength before heading to the hospital. A favorite and fitting passage came to her mind. She turned to Matthew 5:16 and read *"Let your light so shine before men, that they may see your good works, and glorify your Father which is in heaven."*

Anna paused a moment to meditate on that verse and how it applied to this situation she was about to face. She was filled with compassion and hoped Bonnie would credit God as the source of this virtue.

After returning her Bible to her purse, Anna prayed, *"Father God, Please prepare Bonnie's heart that it may be open to receive your love. I trust that you are in control. Thank you for your Word and precious promises. Thank you that your healing hand is at work in Bonnie's body, mind and spirit. In Jesus' name, Amen."*

19

"Mom?" Rebecca spoke softly into the phone.

"Rebecca? Is that you, darling?" her mother, Eva, asked with a mix of elation and concern.

"Yes, it's me," Rebecca whimpered.

"It is so good to hear your voice, sweetie," her mother sighed with relief.

"You too," Rebecca confessed followed by a lull of silence. "I've messed up, Mom."

"What do you mean?" her mother asked.

"Nothing is working out here. I just want to quit and come home," she begged.

"Oh, Rebecca. You are so close to summer break. Why don't you come home for a weekend visit to refresh and then go back and finish the semester?" her mother suggested.

"I don't know," Rebecca replied.

"Please, Rebecca. We love you and miss you so much. A visit will be good for all of us."

"I'll think about it, Mom," Rebecca said. "I have to go now. I love you. Tell Dad I love him too."

"I love you, Rebecca. *So* much. Goodbye, dear," her mom poured out.

Rebecca slowly hung up the phone. She didn't realize how homesick she was until she heard her mother's sweet voice.

Curling up on her loveseat, she was content to just lay still in the quiet of her apartment. In a short time, she peacefully drifted off to sleep.

Emma had this Thursday off from work just as she typically did ever other week. However today felt different. Instead of resting and rejuvenating, Emma was wrought with worry. Suspecting she was being watched, Emma kept the blinds drawn and the lights off to make it appear as though she was not home. The darkness of her apartment only intensified her fear and angst. *I thought Jake was gone, out of my life.*

Emma tried to keep busy cleaning and organizing. Her nesting stage was in full swing now. The nursery was her favorite room to spruce. As she looked about her baby's room, she grew even fonder of her theme choice. She could picture her sweet baby sleeping in his crib as the wee lamb mobile spun over his head. Placing her right hand under her big belly, she eased herself back into the rocker to take a small break.

"Knock, knock, knock," came a light tap at the front door.

Emma's heart raced at the sound of the knocking. *Jake? Jake!*

"Knock, knock, knock."

She crept down the hall and positioned herself in front of the living room window to the left of the front door. Carefully, she separated the slats of the mini-blind and peaked out to see who was there.

Brenda! Emma threw open the door and gently pulled Brenda in by her left wrist. "What are you doing here?" she asked. "It could be dangerous."

Brenda brought out a business card from her jacket pocket and firmly pushed it into Emma's hand. "Here. Call this number. My brother is an attorney. I already spoke to him. You need help." Brenda insisted.

"I can't afford an attorney!" Emma choked.

"Don't worry about that. He wants to help you," Brenda reassured her.

"Well, ok. I will give him a call then," Emma promised. "Thank you."

"I have to run. I am working the 10am-6pm shift today," Brenda explained.

The young ladies hugged then parted ways. Emma shut and locked the door right after Brenda left. She pulled on the knob multiple times to make sure the lock was working. Staring at the card in her hand, she made a decision to follow through on Brenda's advice. *I will call. Today.*

Matt left the Chrysalis Center at 12:30pm allowing plenty of time to arrive before his 2pm interview. He wore a dark gray suit and white dress shirt with a yellow and blue necktie. His hair style looked fresh and clean compliments of the barber who offers free services on site once a week.

Driving the family car was a real treat for Matt. Usually Maggie had the car on week days while Matt remained at the center searching for jobs on the internet. Several laptops were available in the career development office which was open to the residents seven days a week. The policy was first come, first serve and one hour increments at a time. Much of Matt's typical day was spent going back and forth to take another turn on a computer. He knew that it took many, many applications to generate just one interview.

Although Matt fully realized the pressure that came with today's interview, he purposed not to let it bother him. He reached for the radio and flipped through the stations to find some soothing music. Before long, a familiar melody filled the air and Matt began to sing. His voice rose loud as he belted out lyrics he hadn't sung since childhood.

His mind drifted to an earlier time in his life, a simpler time. The hymn brought back wonderful memories of attending morning church services with Granny Nina and Grampy Tim. Summers in their country home were a welcome respite from the shuffling that came with being raised by divorced parents.

Matt would be forever grateful to Granny and Grampy for modeling a loving home and marriage to him. *They loved each other so much.* He could still picture them in their modest kitchen. There was Granny Nina serving Grampy Tim a slice of peach pie with a glass of cold milk in a little red plastic cup. And of course, she would never serve up any dish to her husband without a tender kiss. Even after forty some odd years of marriage, they were like newlyweds up to their passing a few years ago.

But it was their love of God that Matt remembered most. After supper, they would sit on their back porch and read their Bibles while the sun set. Their Bibles were so worn, written in from cover to cover. Sometimes they would even read scripture out loud to each other like other couples do a newspaper or magazine. *They were special alright.*

He didn't want the memories of those summers to end. But this was it. Matt had arrived at his destination. He parked his car in the designated parking lot and turned off the engine. He looked at his watch. 1:30pm. Still time for preparation.

That was when he remembered.

It was the summer after his thirteenth birthday. One Sunday in late July, Matt walked straight down the aisle of Canton Community Church and made a commitment to God in front of Preacher Paul, Granny Nina, Grampy Tim and the entire congregation. He asked Jesus to forgive him of all his sins and to be his personal Lord and Savior. Granny Nina said it was just like getting a new birthday and a new best friend.

In the midst of this poignant memory, a peace came over Matt, just like it had when he was thirteen. All these years, he had forgotten about his best friend.

Right there, in the driver's seat of the family vehicle, a repentant Matt prayed out loud to the very God that saved him that summer. *"Jesus, forgive me for leaving you. I need you now more than ever. Help me make things right with you and for my family. I recommit my life to you today. In your name, Amen."*

Matt took a deep breath and exhaled slowly. The clock on the dashboard read 1:45pm. Time to go. *Now, I am ready.* Matt grinned and stepped out of his car, a new man. A memory verse from a Sunday school class long ago popped into his mind. He recited it boldly as he strode confidently through the parking lot to his interview. *"I can do all things through Christ who strengtheneth me."* Philippians 4:13

––––––––––––

Bonnie was sleeping when Anna came into the room. The heavy curtains were drawn making the time seem more like midnight instead of only four o'clock in the afternoon. Anna decided to stand by Bonnie's bed for awhile before taking a seat in the adjacent blue vinyl chair. She made herself comfortable as she was committed to remain by Bonnie's side for however long she was called to stay.

Anna carefully removed a small Bible from her quilted tote bag. She held the little black book with both hands and raised it up eye level. Her gaze was fixed. Her grip was tight. It was as if this book was life itself to her. *And to Bonnie.*

Instinctively, she opened it up just left of center and began to read aloud in a soft, but authoritative voice. *"The Lord is my Shepherd; I shall not want. He maketh me to lie down in green pastures: he leadeth me beside the still waters."* Psalms 23: 1-3

Bonnie began to stir. Anna continued to quietly read aloud.

"He restoreth my soul: he leadeth me in the paths of righteousness for his name's sake. Yea, though I walk through the valley of the shadow of death, I will fear no evil: for thou art with me; thy rod and thy staff they comfort me." Psalms 23:4

Bonnie rolled on her side to face Anna. She blinked slowly trying to wake up, but could not hold open her eyes. Anna went on, *"Thou preparest a table before me in the presence of mine enemies; thou anointest my head with oil; my cup runneth over. Surely goodness and mercy shall follow me all the days of my life: and I will dwell in the house of the Lord for ever."* Psalms 23:5

Anna pulled down the attached satin book mark to keep her place as she slowly closed her Bible. After returning her Bible to her tote bag, Anna scooted her chair closer to Bonnie's bed.

Anna placed her hand on top of Bonnie's and caressed it gently. Fully awake now, Bonnie smiled brightly at her visitor.

"Bonnie!" Anna cheered. "How are you feeling?"

"Tired, but ok," Bonnie replied. "What was that you were reading? It sounded so familiar, but I couldn't place it?"

"It was from the Bible," Anna explained, "the 23rd Psalm."

"Yes. That's it!" Bonnie recalled out loud.

91

Just then the door opened suddenly. Two men and one woman entered the room in a hurried and deliberate manner. While one of the men wore blue scrubs, the other two wore the traditional white apparel. All three wore serious expressions as they lined up at the foot of Bonnie's bed.

"Ms. Franklin, we have the results of your tests. You have a growth on your heart. The growth causes your heart to work harder than it was designed to work. That extra work contributed to your recent heart attack. If it is not removed, you could have another one. And the next one could be fatal," Dr. May informed Bonnie.

"We will also be testing the growth itself to determine whether it is benign or malignant," Dr. Aru added.

Neither Bonnie nor Anna said a word. Anna tightened her grip on Bonnie's hand.

"There is a risk of rupturing the heart when removing the growth," explained Dr. May. "But the alternative of doing nothing is more risky."

Anna asked, "When would you operate?"

"Tuesday, 11am," Dr. Aru answered. "There are a few more tests to do. And there is a surgeon from the Cleveland Clinic who specializes in this procedure. He has agreed to perform the operation. He will arrive Monday."

Bonnie remained silent and still. She made eye contact briefly with Anna then turned her attention back to her team of doctors.

Dr. May asserted, "We will check back with you in one hour to obtain your permission to schedule."

Then as quickly as they entered and changed Bonnie's world, the doctors left without so much as a look back. *Oh, how life can change so fast. Just like that.*

20

Rebecca headed to Anna's extra early Monday hoping to catch her before her fellow students showed up for class. It was 4:30pm when she arrived and class didn't start until 6pm. Worried she was inappropriate by her early arrival; Rebecca nervously climbed the porch stairs and approached the front door. Her heart was racing a bit, second guessing her decision.

She knocked, lightly; half hoping Anna would not answer so she could just come back later and not go through with her plan. But almost immediately, Anna peered through the Palladian window at the top of her door. Her eyes brightened when she saw Rebecca. At once, Anna opened the door wide as she wiped her hands on a white apron that hung around her neck.

"Rebecca!" Anna exclaimed. "Good to see you!" Without hesitation, Anna took Rebecca by the hand and pulled her inside. She gave Rebecca a big bear hug, something they both were in need of.

"Come. Sit down." Anna led the way to her sitting room and pointed to a deep, overstuffed chair in the corner adjacent to a matching sofa. Rebecca took a seat in the cozy chair while Anna sat down on the sofa and scooted to the side closest to her guest.

Anna turned to Rebecca and asked her directly, "What is going on?"

"Oh, Anna. My life is a mess." Tears rolled down Rebecca's cheeks.

Anna reached for Rebecca's hands and clasped them with her own, one on top and one underneath. "I am here for you. Tell me what brings your tears?"

"I don't know where to start," Rebecca sniffled. "I am ashamed of myself and the things I have done."

Anna tightened the grip on Rebecca's hands to offer reassurance. "Go on," Anna pressed her to continue.

"I drink every night, Anna. And I do things that I regret. Sometimes I do not even remember what happens." Rebecca sobbed and pulled her hands in to cover her face. "I am so scared."

Rebecca took a deep breath and began again. "I just wanted to make friends. I went to a party here and then a happy hour there. I was lonely. And I wanted to find love."

Anna stroked Rebecca's hair softly with her hand, but didn't say a word.

"Anna, I would only drink beer. No liquor, so I thought it was so innocent. But now I can't go a day without drinking. I am starting to drink earlier and earlier every day, sometimes right after lunch."

"What else?" Anna probed.

"I am sick. Always exhausted, irritable, sad," Rebecca described herself. "And my grades are dropping."

"There is still something else, isn't there?" Anna's instincts told her.

"I have certainly not found love either. Just the opposite actually. I made a huge mistake, unfixable." Rebecca confessed. "I believe I lost my virginity."

"You believe?" Anna asked.

"I woke up one morning in bed with a guy from my biology class." Rebecca confessed. "Oh, Anna. The details about the night are so fuzzy."

"Rebecca, come sit over here by me," Anna requested in a commanding voice while patting the couch cushion next to her.

Rebecca recognized that Anna's serious tone conflicted with the compassion in her eyes. Trusting her instincts, Rebecca decided to join Anna on the sofa. Her head hung low as she slowly took the seat beside her teacher, her friend. Anna turned and wrapped her arms around Rebecca's limp, worn body. Rebecca collapsed hard into Anna's loving embrace and let go of all her pain.

Struggling to catch her breath between sobs, Rebecca's heart continued to break as she relived her mistakes in her mind. When she could cry no longer, Rebecca settled into Anna's arms and rested silently for several minutes. Gradually she lifted her tear streaked face and looked into Anna's eyes.

"Do you want a fresh start, honey?" Anna asked.

"If only there was a way," Rebecca responded desperately.

"There *is* a way," Anna spoke confidently.

"How?"

"Rebecca, we have all made mistakes," Anna began. "You can be forgiven of all those mistakes and have a new beginning. God, our heavenly Father, loves you so much. Our mistakes, called sin, separate us from God. He has provided a way to remove that separation and have a love relationship with Him."

Rebecca scrunched her brows as she listened intently to Anna's words.

Anna continued sharing, "God sent His son, Jesus, to earth. Jesus was both God and man. He took the punishment for our sins by dying on the cross. After three days, Jesus rose from the dead. See, Jesus, took our place. When we trust in Jesus, our relationship with God is restored."

"What do you mean.....trust in Jesus?" Rebecca inquired.

"A love relationship with God begins with trust. You let go, surrender; trust your life to God. You exchange the plans you have for your life for God's plan," Anna explained.

"How do you do *that*?" asked Rebecca.

"Believe that Jesus is God's Son, that He was born on earth, died on the cross in your place personally and that He resurrected from the dead."

"I do believe that," Rebecca confirmed.

"Ask God to forgive you of your sins and accept that forgiveness. Turn from your sins and live for God," Anna instructed.

"I don't know how to change, Anna. I have already tried and failed," Rebecca expressed.

"When you ask Jesus to be your personal Lord and Savior and invite Him into your heart, He does the changing!!!! God will fill you with His Holy Spirit who will comfort you, guide you, and give you power to live for Him."

"I need a new life," Rebecca surrendered. "I need a Savior."

"Rebecca, do you want to pray with me now and experience love and peace like you have never known?" Anna asked.

"Yes," Rebecca committed.

Anna and Rebecca joined hands. "Pray after me."

Rebecca nodded.

Anna prayed, *"Dear God, I am a sinner. I believe that Jesus, your son, died on a cross to pay for my sins and that He rose from the dead. Please forgive me of my sins and save me. Jesus, I ask you to come into my heart and be my personal Savior and Lord of my life. Thank you for loving me and for your Spirit living in me now. In Jesus' name, Amen."*

Rebecca repeated the prayer word for word, slowly and deliberately. After they prayed together, Anna hugged Rebecca and welcomed her, "Rebecca, you have been born again. *This* time into *God's* family. A brand new life."

A huge smile spread across Rebecca's face. "Does that make us *sisters*?" she squealed jokingly.

"As a matter of fact, it does!" Anna confirmed. "You now have a physical family *and* a spiritual family."

"Thank you for being there for me, Anna," Rebecca stated sincerely.

"Don't you mean, *sister*?" Anna corrected with a chuckle.

Tears of despair turned to happiness that Monday afternoon. Anna was overjoyed that Rebecca gave her heart to Jesus. *Such good news! The Good News! Indeed!*

21

"Now what?" Rebecca questioned.

Having already gone to one of her crowded book shelves, Anna handed Rebecca a black leather book. The *Good Book* as Anna's mother used to call it. "Rebecca, here is a Bible. It is God's Holy Word. Read it every day. It will teach you all about your new Christian life and how to live it victoriously."

"I will," Rebecca promised.

"Pray every day and often. Talk to God about anything and everything. Be sure to take time to be still and listen in your heart for his direction."

"Attend church regularly. One that teaches the Bible and overflows with love. You may visit the church I belong if you would like?" invited Anna.

"Be deliberate in meeting and developing friendships with other Christians. They will encourage you in your walk with the Lord," Anna continued to disciple Rebecca.

"Be sure to tell others what God has done for you and that He wants to extend the same love and forgiveness to them too," Anna stressed emphatically.

"This is so exciting!" Rebecca rejoiced.

Anna agreed, "It has only just begun."

Emma and Maggie spotted each other as they pulled in along the curb in front of Anna's traditional colonial style home. Even in the midst of winter, 206 Albert always seemed bright and cheery, radiating its own sunshine in the long, bleak season typical of Western Ohio. The two women exchanged friendly glances as they stepped out of their vehicles shutting their car doors at almost the same time. Maggie parked closest to Anna's walkway and politely waited for Emma to meet up with her.

"Hello!" Maggie called out when Emma was just a short distance away. Emma returned the greeting with a smile and quickened her pace.

"Hi," said Emma. "How are you?"

"Good. Yourself?" Maggie asked.

"Great," Emma answered.

Good. Great. Mere formalities. Neither description being accurate. But both women decided it best to hide their troubles, looking forward to spending an evening of escape.

"Come on in from the bitter cold," Rebecca shouted out to Emma and Maggie as they made their way up the wooden stairs to Anna's porch. They were careful to hold on tight to the hand rails knowing the evening temperatures caused ice to form on nearly every exposed surface.

Rebecca held open the front door while her fellow students rushed inside, anxious to partake in the warmth that was such a stark contrast from the frigid weather outside. After scurrying in from the elements, Emma and Maggie stomped their feet hard on a bristled mat in the foyer to rid their soles of any snow.

"Good to see you," Rebecca said. "Anna is upstairs. She asked me to let you in and show you to the sewing room. Follow me!"

Emma and Maggie slipped off their boots and followed Rebecca through the hall and into the first room on the right. While waiting for their teacher, the women mingled about trading light conversation. They made themselves at home arranging a few hard backed chairs into a circle near the bay window. The lively chatter never lulled as Rebecca, Maggie and Emma sat down in anticipation of the night's lesson.

Minutes later, Anna appeared in the doorway carrying a silver tray that held a small ceramic teapot, matching teacups and white linen napkins. She paused briefly and nodded to her guests before heading straight for the large cutting table in the center of the room. Steadily, she placed the tray down and began pouring. "Tea?" she offered.

"Yes."

"Oh, please."

"Thank you."

All three agreed and accepted the hot treat as their gracious host took turns serving them one by one. Once her guests were served, she poured herself a tea and took a seat in the group.

Anna looked especially beautiful tonight. Elegant, actually. She wore a pale pink long sleeved blouse tucked into a solid gray skirt that flowed down to just above her ankles. Her hair was tied back loosely with a wide black satin ribbon that coordinated perfectly with her pretty, yet practical black slipper shoes.

"Where's Bonnie?" Maggie asked.

Caught off guard in the middle of her first sip, Anna peered over top of her rim realizing Maggie's question was directed at her. Slowly, she brought her teacup down from her mouth and carefully held it on her lap with both hands.

"Bonnie is in the hospital. Heart attack. She is being operated on tomorrow. 11am," Anna reported.

Gasps of disbelief filled the air. "Oh, no," Emma shared her concern.

"She will be joining us again real soon," Anna promised. There was a confidence in Anna's voice that put the group at ease.

"I am sure she will," Rebecca added. The ladies nodded in unison signifying their agreement with Anna's prognosis.

Several moments of silence passed before Anna rose and began class. She stationed the women in different areas of the room depending on the stage of their projects. Soon their busy hands took the place of their busy thoughts, giving their minds a temporary diversion.

Anna gave individual instruction as she walked each student through their particular step. Rebecca was pinning a pattern to fabric for her tote bag. Maggie was cutting material for her placemats, carefully following the outline that she marked with white pencil the prior class. Emma was seated at one of the sewing machines ready to begin stitching together the sides of her baby blanket.

As Anna stood back and watched the ladies concentrating on their tasks at hand, it became clear to her that she was in the center of God's will. She was experiencing a perfect peace knowing her life had intercepted exactly with God's plan for her.

I love you, Jesus, Anna prayed in her heart. *I love you.*

22

Emma's legs were shaking as she sat in the waiting room of Cross, Hadley and Stone. A voice mail message left from Jake last night on her home phone convinced Emma the time had come to face the truth. She was in danger, possibly eminent. Emma barely slept all night, keeping one ear on the door, the other on the windows, scared Jake would be bold enough to break in. She watched and waited for the digital clock in her bedroom to turn 8:00am, a reasonable hour she figured to make her phone call. Taking her co-worker's advice, Emma called the telephone number to Brenda's brother's law firm to request an appointment. After explaining the purpose of her call, the receptionist urged her to come in right away.

It was 9am, Tuesday, February 15th, just over three months until her baby was due. Here she sat planning a divorce when she really wished she was planning her baby shower instead. Her heart ached as waves of reality hit her, drowning her thoughts. First fear, then anger. Fear, then anger. Yes, she was angry with Jake, but more so, she was angry with herself. She vowed to spend the rest of her life being the best mother, to try and make up to her child for the chaotic circumstances she was responsible for creating.

Emma swallowed hard to fight back public tears. Determined to bring her emotions in check, she grabbed a

107

magazine from the credenza next to her. She flipped the glossy pages, one after another, rapid and rough. Though never stopping to read an article, the flashy pictures caught her attention long enough to shift her focus and settle her nerves before meeting with Ken Cross.

"Mrs. Rhoades?" A tall, thin, blonde gentleman in a sharp black suit was standing before her extending his hand.

"Yes." Emma stood and shook his hand, noticing his firm grip. His baby blue eyes seemed to look right through her. In that moment, if only for a moment, Emma felt safe.

I am glad I came here. Emma thought. *Very glad.*

"Matt, shouldn't you have heard something by now?" Maggie snapped anxious to hear about her husband's interview. She pushed her lukewarm scrambled eggs around on her plate and then tapped her fork on the edge waiting impatiently for Matt's answer.

"I am sure I will today, Maggie," he assured her.

"We have to be out day after next," Maggie reminded him sadly.

Matt nodded, but didn't say anything. He needed no reminder.

"I have my things packed." Maggie paused and waited for a response.

Matt remained silent. As he listened to his wife's words, Matt prayed fervently in his heart and mind asking God for a miracle.

"I will pack the children's things tonight after I get back from work," she planned aloud.

"Maggie, try not to worry. God is in control," Matt promised.

"God? *GOD?*" Maggie jumped up at stared at Matt with angry eyes. "Uuuuhhh!" She huffed, turned and stormed out of the dining hall leaving her dirty tray behind, and her husband.

Matt did not expect that strong of a reaction from Maggie. From old habit, his first instinct was to run after her like he did whenever they got into an argument. This time was different. He was different.

He emptied both of their cafeteria trays and quickly left the dining hall with a conversation or two on his mind. First God, then Maggie.

Matt knew God would listen anytime, anyplace, anywhere. But he craved a place where he could get alone before God. Privacy was hard to come by at the Chrysalis Center. Then he remembered a private room down the employment hallway where residents could have phone interviews, reservations only.

Matt took his chances. Unoccupied, the sign read. Relieved, Matt hurried to the intake desk to see if he could use the room for a bit.

"Fifteen minutes," the clerk admonished and handed him a key. "Don't make me come get you."

"No, ma'am," Matt agreed.

The clerk eyed him like a child, never seeing so much excitement for a phone interview. Matt ignored her curious look and headed for the room. Once inside, he gently shut the door and decided not to turn on the lights. *Awwwh.* The room was dim, but not dark as light crept in from the hall.

As he reached into his pocket to turn off his cell phone, he chuckled thinking how funny to have no phone in the phone room. Even in the midst of crisis, Matt had joy.

Matt fell to his knees and sat back on his heels. With open eyes, he lifted his head and face skyward, toward heaven. He turned his palms up and lifted them shoulder high.

"Father God," Matt began to pray aloud. *"Thank you for bringing me back to you. Thank you for forgiving me of turning away from you for so long. You are truly a loving father."* Matt paused overtaken by the reality of how unconditionally God loved him, personally. *"I desire to be a Godly husband and father. I need to provide my family a home, a place where they can feel secure and loved. I need a fresh start. Please, Father. I need your help, today. I trust you to answer my prayer according to your will. In your son, Jesus' name, Amen."*

23

The below freezing temperatures and early morning hour did not keep Rebecca from meeting Anna in the lobby of Dayton General Hospital. It was 6:30am. Enough time to visit Bonnie before her 11am surgery.

Waking up this early was a far cry from Rebecca's usual time, which on good days was noon. As a matter of fact, it was not uncommon for Rebecca to be just rolling home about now. But Anna told Rebecca last night that upon her confession of faith, things would be different.

Rebecca was a Christian for less than twenty four hours, yet she had already begun to understand what Anna meant by being born again. Anna explained that she had a new life now, in Christ.

While glancing up at a large clock on the wall, Rebecca rejoiced inside over her decision to accept Jesus. 6:30 Am. 6:30AM! *Yes, this surely is a new life!* She proclaimed silently to herself.

A tap on her right shoulder shook Rebecca from her sweet reverie. As she turned, Anna cheerfully greeted her, "Good morning!"

"Good morning to you," Rebecca returned.

The ladies gave each other a quick hug and then set out on their way to Bonnie's room. Energetic and deliberate, they hustled through the main floor to the separate elevator lobby. The ride to the third floor was fast and smooth. Outside Bonnie's room was a rolling metal cart filled with clipboards and charts, along with an array of medical supplies. Her door was ajar allowing Rebecca and Anna to peer in unnoticed.

A nurse was standing over Bonnie appearing to be adjusting an intravenous needle. Anna knocked on the door lightly while quietly asking the nurse permission to enter.

"Certainly," the young woman dressed in white replied. "Come in."

"Thank you," Anna said graciously as she walked slowly into the room with Rebecca close behind her.

"I am done here for now," the nurse shared. "Enjoy your visit. I will be back in about forty five minutes to move Bonnie to prep."

The women nodded to the nurse and then moved along side Bonnie's bed. Anna took Bonnie's hand and asked, "How are you?"

"Scared," Bonnie answered, eyes glistening with tears.

Rebecca laid her hand on top of Anna's for additional support. "We miss you, Bonnie. And we can't wait for you to be back in class," Rebecca expressed with high hopes.

Bonnie barely nodded, cautious of committing to the future.

Anna wasted no time in turning the conversation serious. "Bonnie, no one is promised tomorrow. No one."

Rebecca was surprised by Anna's opening sentence, but knew it to be true. She listened intently as Anna proceeded in explaining the reality of eternity. When we die, we will either spend eternity with God in heaven or apart from God in hell."

"Bonnie, I know you are afraid," Anna acknowledged.

"I am afraid. What if I do not make it through the operation?" Bonnie admitted.

"You do not have to fear death. You can know for sure you will go to heaven when you die," Anna said confidently.

"God created you. He wants fellowship with you forever, both here on earth and heaven," Anna explained.

"I have been a good person, Anna. I think I would go to heaven," Bonnie defended.

"Bonnie, the Bible says in the book of Titus, chapter 3, verses 5 and 6 that it is *'Not by works of righteousness which we have done, but according to his mercy he saved us, by the washing of regeneration, and renewing of the Holy Ghost; which he shed on us abundantly through Jesus Christ our Saviour,'* Anna quoted from memory.

"Bonnie, you cannot earn your way into heaven. The gift of eternal life with God is free. That is why it is called a gift," Anna described.

"You see, sin, which is all the wrong and hurtful things we say and do, separates us from God," Anna continued. "We are all sinners. Only one person ever lived a sinless life and that is Jesus Christ, God's son."

"God loves you so much that he made a way to remove that separation. He sent his son to earth, born a baby to a virgin named Mary. Jesus, being both God and human, died on a cross taking the punishment for our sins. He paid the price for our sin. Our debt is paid in full by Jesus' sacrifice. He was buried in a tomb and after three days He rose from the dead."

"The Bible says in the book of John, chapter 3, verse 16, *"For God so loved the world, that He gave His only begotten Son, that whosoever believeth in Him should not perish, but have everlasting life."*

"Whosoever. *Who*soever," Anna emphasized. "Bonnie, you can be one of the whosoever and have the assurance of everlasting life."

Though Bonnie did not yet speak, her body relaxed and her eyes softened, the Holy Spirit at work in her.

"Bonnie, would you like to know for certain, without a doubt, that if you were to die you would go to heaven?" Anna asked directly.

"Yes."

"The Bible says in the book of Romans, chapter 10, verse 9 *'That if thou shalt confess with thy mouth the Lord Jesus, and shalt believe in thine heart that God hath raised him from the dead, thou shalt be saved.'* "

"Bonnie, would you like to pray with me now to accept Jesus and invite him to live in your heart?" Anna confirmed Bonnie's intentions before moving on.

"Oh, yes."

"Pray these words after me and believe them in your heart."
Anna, Bonnie, and Rebecca all joined hands and bowed their
heads.

*"Dear God, I know I am a sinner. I am sorry for my sins.
Please forgive me. I believe that Jesus, your son, came to earth
and died on a cross to take the punishment for my sins. I believe
that after three days He rose from the dead. Jesus, save me. I
invite you into my heart to be my personal Savior and Lord of my
life. Thank you for your love and for your Holy Spirit that lives
inside me now. In Jesus' name, Amen."*

Bonnie repeated each word, annunciating every syllable
slowly and clearly. Her voice filled with overwhelming
thanksgiving as she experienced the presence of God and a
lifting of her life long loneliness.

Tears of relief poured from Bonnie's eyes with no signs of
stopping. She tightened her grip on Anna and Rebecca's hands
as if holding still this moment in time. Too precious to let go.

The sounds of Bonnie's sniffles and gasps for air between
sobs drowned out most of the noise from the monitors attached
to her body. The experience being surreal and beautiful, yet in
the background chirped on the repetitive beep of equipment and
machines of all kinds. A reminder that though her physical life
hung in the balance, her spiritual life was secure.

Anna was first to release hands, breaking free to get a tissue
from a box on the bedside table. She blotted Bonnie's face dry,

115

patting her skin so gently and lovingly. While Rebecca took her hand and pushed Bonnie's bangs back from her eyes.

"Bonnie, I am here for you," Rebecca committed.

"Thank you," Bonnie managed to say as her emotions began to steady; adjusting to the exchange from despair to hope.

"Just last night, I accepted Jesus too!" Rebecca shared. "We are sisters now. Sisters in Christ!"

"I like the sound of that!" Bonnie smiled. All the women laughed out loud rejoicing together.

"Bonnie, let me pray for you and then we will see you when you get out of surgery."

Anna led her sisters in prayer as she asked the Lord to do a miracle.

"Father God, We love you and trust you. Please be with our sister, Bonnie. Guide the surgeon's hands, allow the growth on her heart to be removed easily and without complication, may the test results return benign, grant her a quick and speedy recovery and complete healing. We thank you for Bonnie's salvation today and for the Holy Spirit to fill her as she walks in her new life. In Jesus' name, Amen."

Anna and Rebecca left the room together and walked to the nearest waiting room. There they sat next to each other on a small vinyl couch. Quietly and patiently they waited, anticipating a good report in a few hours of their friend's outcome. When the Holy Spirit brought a verse to Anna's remembrance, she whispered it softly to Rebecca to disciple her on the Lord's way to wait, *"Rejoice evermore. Pray without ceasing. In every thing give thanks: for this is the will of God in Christ Jesus concerning you."* *1 Thessalonians 5:16-18*

24

Ken Cross escorted his new client into his office and gestured for her to take a seat. The office was grand, but comfortable, decorated nicely with rich colors and fine furnishings. There were two leather high backed chairs arranged across from a traditional executive style desk. Emma chose the one closest to the door. *Easy out*, she thought, just in case it all became too much for her.

Once Emma was seated, the attorney walked behind the desk and sat down to begin their meeting. Emma remained quiet while Mr. Cross opened his side drawer and pulled out a yellow legal pad, placing it on his otherwise empty desk. Next, he retrieved an elegant silver pen from inside his suit jacket pocket and jotted a brief note at the top of the pad.

The clutter free surroundings made Emma feel important, as though his focus was solely on her situation. She fidgeted in her chair, knowing his coming questions would not be easy.

"Mrs. Rhoades, I can help you," Mr. Cross started out, nodding his head assuredly.

Emma listened closely, hanging on his words.

"Indeed, this is a very difficult time right now. But there will be a day again that you will wake up without fear and be able to smile at your future," he claimed confidently.

Emma believed, or at least wanted to believe, this man was making her an actual promise. Tears trickled out the corners of her eyes at the mere possibility of his promise coming true.

Mr. Cross responded quickly to Emma. Twisting and leaning back hard to his right, he stretched to reach a box of tissues from off a shelf of the bookcase behind him. After offering her a tissue, he placed the box on his desk, near the front edge, arm length from her.

"Thank you," Emma said, dabbing her tears, pulling herself together.

"No, Mrs. Rhoades. Thank *you* for the opportunity to help," Mr. Cross returned.

An hour turned into almost two before their meeting wrapped up. Emma explained her journey, the ups and downs, and where she hoped to go from this point. She left the law office just after 11am, in far better shape than she arrived. Plans were in motion.

No, Ken Cross. Thank you. Emma insisted in her heart. *Thank you.*

———————————

Matt waited impatiently in the lobby of the Chrysalis Center for his wife to arrive home from work Tuesday afternoon. Home, yes, *home*. The shelter on the corner of Fourth and Main has been home to the Tucker family now for fifty eight days with the cap being sixty. The waiting list being so long in the city, their extension request was denied.

In between pacing the floor, Matt would try and sit for awhile to help pass the time. His right leg would bounce nearly non-stop until all he could do was get up and pace some more.

It was almost 4:30pm now. *Where was Maggie? Her shift ended at 3:00pm. Where were the children? Their bus should have dropped them off an hour ago.*

Matt called Maggie's cell phone. *Voicemail.* Minutes later, he tried again. *Voicemail.*

"Ladies," a man, a surgeon, walked into the waiting room and addressed Anna and Rebecca.

"Yes," confirmed Anna, both women springing to their feet.

"Your friend, Bonnie, is doing great," the doctor announced. "The growth on her heart was completely removed without any damage to the outer tissue. Preliminary tests show that the growth was benign. We will do further testing, but I see no evidence that the results will be different."

"Oh, praise God!" Anna squealed. "Thank you, Doctor."

The doctor smiled and nodded his head before leaving the waiting area.

Anna and Rebecca hugged tightly rejoicing in the good news. *Good news! God news!*

SLAM! Maggie jerked and looked back when the heavy steel entrance door slammed shut. A blast of icy air followed in behind them as they entered the Wright Now Women's Center on Berlin Avenue.

"Come on in out of that cold!" commanded a loud voice with a heavy Spanish accent. Seconds later, a short dark haired woman rushed out from a side office.

"Please, come in," she repeated herself.

"Thank you," replied a worn and weary Maggie Tucker, her two children in tow. Before moving closer, she marched in place a few times on a rubber mat to shake the slush off her boots.

"Hi. I'm Olga."

"I am Maggie Tucker and these are my two children, Abigail and Andrew."

When Maggie extended her hand to shake, Olga ignored the gesture and gave her a big bear hug instead.

Olga pulled back and asked, "What brings you here, honey?"

Maggie took a deep breath, then explained, "You see, my family and I have been staying at the Chrysalis Center for almost two months after we lost our home. Our stay is up day after next."

"And you need a place to go?" Olga surmised.

"Yes, ma'am."

"We are full today, dear. But we may have an opening in a day or so. There is a possibility of a check out on Thursday."

"Oh," was all Maggie could find the strength to say.

122

"May I have a contact number for you? I will know for sure tomorrow and call you," Olga promised.

"Thank you. My cell number is 513-555-2148." Maggie took the children by the hand and left the shelter.

Summoning courage, Maggie opened the back car door as her sweet children clamored in.

Where will we go? Where can we turn? Dusk was approaching. Fog settling in. Hard to see ahead. *Like her life.* She thought. *Just like her life.*

25

Emma was glad she decided to call in to work this morning. But she still had a twinge of guilt leftover from waking her boss, Kathy, at 6am to let her know. She dutifully followed hotel procedure, calling her supervisor two hours before her start time. The news came with little pressure since Emma arranged the night before to have Brenda cover her shift. Although this was just the second day she missed during her pregnancy, guilt continued to nag her even into the evening.

Kathy was an excellent boss; intelligent, motivating, and kind. Emma wanted to please her. Actually, Emma just wanted to please period. Somewhere along the way, trying to please went from a habit to a lifestyle. For so long she tried to please Jake, to win his affection. Before Jake, it was Tom in high school, before that, her father. Before that, well, she couldn't remember a before that.

Her intentions were simple. To be liked. No, to be loved. The irony is, the harder she tried to please, the less loved she felt. She did not notice that her self-dignity was being chipped away with every compromise she made in contradiction to her conscience.

Until what remained of her was but a shell of a girl. The pain of rejection like grains of sand in her soul that rubbed together over and over. Tears of lost love washed through the shell of her existence and over the pain. Yet out of all these emotions something, *someone*, of great worth was forming. *A pearl. Her baby.*

It was 6pm before Maggie and the children reached the Chrysalis Center, well past their normal arrival time. Matt was wrought with worry, unable to reach Maggie by cell phone all afternoon. He was standing at the front door stationed like a soldier when he spotted his family walking up the sidewalk toward him.

Maggie, caught off guard by his presence, took a step backward when she first laid eyes on her husband. Her instinct was to retreat; half mad, half embarrassed by her own behavior.

But much to Maggie's surprise, Matt ran to meet her. He grabbed her and hugged her frantically. Then he kissed her tenderly on her lips, long and sweet.

"I love you, Maggie Tucker. I am so glad you are here," Matt exclaimed.

"Oh, Matt, I love you," Maggie returned, feeling secure in his arms.

"Abigail and Andrew, I love you so much too." Matt knelt down on his right knee and gathered his daughter and son into his arms, hugging them both at the same time.

"We love you too, Daddy," the children repeated one at a time.

"Let's go inside," Matt rallied the troops.

The couple wrapped their arms around each other's backs and walked side by side into the shelter. Their cherubs following close behind.

Once inside, Matt shared the miracle. *The miracle.* Yes. The events of this day would always be known to Matt as *the miracle.*

Rebecca tried to steady her hands by tightening her grip on the steering wheel. Her stomach cramped before a rush of nausea. She tried to ignore the obvious. Her heart pounded in her chest. She recognized the signs all too well. Rebecca needed a drink.

The next intersection was crucial. A left turn led to the District with its upscale night clubs, bistros, and bars. A right turn led through downtown to campus. Though filled with its own familiar trappings, campus was home.

She was stopped at the red.

"Oh, God!" she cried out. *"Why is this happening? Help me."*

The traffic light turned green.

Green. The color registered. *Go.* But she froze. *Go where?*

HONK came from behind.

Her cell phone rang. It was an easy grab, right on her lap.

"Hello?" Rebecca answered hastily.

127

"Rebecca, it's me, Anna. I would love to have you over for supper tonight. Are you still in the area?"

HOOOONNNNNKK the driver from behind laid on their horn void of any further patience.

"I will be there in ten minutes. Thank you."

Rebecca drove straight through the intersection. Neither left, nor right.

"Thank you, Lord." Rebecca prayed silently. *"You heard my cry and answered my call."*

Anna dished up some hearty comfort food. Meatloaf with a tangy ketchup crust, mashed potatoes smothered in butter, fresh corn, and dinner rolls right out of the oven. For dessert, she served hot apple tarts topped with vanilla ice cream drizzled with rich caramel syrup.

The ladies ate slowly enjoying good food and good company. Just light conversation and laughter, nothing heavy following their emotionally tense day at the hospital.

After the meal, the friends moved to the den where they stretched out on a long, soft sofa opposite a rustic brick fireplace. The crackling of the fire was all that could be heard in the room. Both women were far too tired and too full to talk much.

"Rebecca, I have made up the guest room for you just in case you were too tired to drive. You are free to spend the night if you like," Anna offered.

"You have done enough already," Rebecca replied graciously.

"My pleasure!"

A quiet night's sleep after a home cooked meal was too good for Rebecca to pass up. "Thank you, Anna. I will take you up on that offer." Rebecca smiled and stood to her feet. "Beginning right now."

"Good night, Rebecca."

"Good night, Anna."

Rebecca turned and left Anna in the quietness of the den. She slowly made her way up the staircase, step by step.

Step by step. That's it! Rebecca knew. *That's how! Step by step.*

26

The light was so bright Bonnie could hardly open her eyes. She blinked and blinked, but still she could not see for the brightness. *Is this heaven?* She wondered. *Am I about to meet my maker?*

Bonnie was relieved when she remembered putting her faith in Jesus yesterday morning. Her memory of that decision recreated those same feelings inside her of love, joy and peace.

She blinked again. This time she could make out a figure. Slowly, her vision came into focus. A woman in white was standing next to a window turning the wand to the mini blind letting in the morning sunshine.

"Good morning, Bonnie!"

An angel? Bonnie considered as her eyes adjusted to her surroundings.

"I am Nurse Kelly. I have been taking care of you this week," the woman explained. "You had a heart operation yesterday."

The pieces were starting to fall into place. Bonnie listened closely.

"You are just now waking up from surgery," Nurse Kelly continued.

Bonnie scrunched her eyebrows and pressed her lips together. She wanted to know the truth. "How did it go?" she asked point blank with a mixture of confidence and caution.

"Great!" Nurse Kelly summed up. "Really great!"

"And the growth on my heart?" she quickly followed up with another question as more details came together for her.

"It was removed without complication and tested benign."

"Wonderful!" celebrated Bonnie. "Like I have a new heart!" *A brand new heart.*

Confused could best describe how Emma felt this dreary Wednesday morning. It was shortly after 9am which constituted sleeping in for the twenty two year old mother-to-be. Her bedroom was still dark even at this hour, typical of mid-winter in western Ohio.

Emma was so grateful to have the day scheduled off, this dreaded day in particular. She knew in just a matter of hours that Jake would be served with divorce papers. As much as she wanted to delay a divorce and hope her husband would change, the time had come to take action. It wasn't safe for her to wait any longer.

She was nervous thinking of his reaction. Would Jake be hurt? Angry? Or would he finally understand consequences? Though she hoped for understanding, she expected anger. Her attorney was prepared at a moment's notice to get a restraining order if necessary.

To take her mind off of things, Emma thought she would run to the fabric store at the Parkway mall. She needed to buy three yards of satin piping before Monday's sewing class to trim her baby blanket.

Emma got out of bed, freshened quickly in the bathroom and threw on a comfy sweatshirt and maternity jeans. Before heading out the door, she sat down at her kitchen table with a strawberry yogurt, whole wheat toast and apple juice. A small breakfast seemed the solution to curb her occasional morning sickness.

Thinking of her baby helped Emma put everything in perspective. Not only was she giving her baby life, her baby was actually giving her life. The more she pondered this realization, this wondrous exchange of life, the more she fell in love with him, or her.

She looked down and placed her hand on her tummy. "I love you," she whispered emphatically. "Before I even know you, I love you." *Oh, I love you.*

After seven months of unemployment, Matt could not bring himself to take a lunch break. But when his new boss invited him directly, he could not refuse. It had been four hours into his new career. *So far, so good,* he thought as he prepared to leave the office shortly for a bite to eat with his new co-workers.

Mr. Craven was a well known and well respected business man in the city. Matt considered it a privilege and honor to work for such a fine gentleman. Craven Residential Communities had been a family business for over forty years. Some of the most affluent neighborhoods in Dayton were developed by Mr. Craven and his company.

Matt's previous project management experience had been in the area of commercial and retail development. So when the call came yesterday offering him a position to oversee building a luxury residential community, Matt thought it had to be divine intervention. But when Mr. Craven requested that he move his family on site and included living in a model home as part of his compensation package, Matt had no further doubt.

It was God. It was *the miracle.* His heavenly Father had answered his prayers. Timely, perfectly, more than Matt ever dreamed possible.

Thank you. He prayed silently in awe of just how much God loved him. *Thank you!*

After Matt shut down his computer and put on his coat, he took a moment to pause as he waited for his group to gather. *The miracle* reminded him of his Granny Rita's favorite scripture, 1 John 4:16 *"God is love."* She used to call it her life verse. He also remembered how she would say God answers all His children's prayers. Sometimes yes, sometimes no, and sometimes wait. But whatever the answer, it is always the right one. Because God *is* love, His answers can only be that of love.

Then Matt thought of Maggie. How he loved her and yearned to share his renewed faith with her. He also yearned to be alone with his wife again, to rekindle the romance and to cause her to fall in love with him again anew. *Tomorrow night, my love, at last tomorrow night.*

"Ready?" Mr. Craven asked jiggling his car keys in his hand.

Matt snapped his attention to his boss and stood to his feet. "Yes, sir. I am ready."

Ready to start my new life, Matt thought bursting with anticipation inside. *More than ready.*

———————————

Thursday morning was check out for the Tucker family. The Chrysalis Center had been their home for the full sixty day cap. Like its name sake, the shelter was a place to stay during a stage of transition in life. It was a place to develop, transform, strengthen and grow wings. Tomorrow was the Tucker's time to fly.

Maggie requested a personal day off from work to coordinate the move. Most of their furnishings were sold over at yard sale until there was nothing left but clothing and a few personal possessions.

With the children at school and Matt at work, Maggie would have the day to herself tomorrow to prepare their homecoming.

She especially wanted to make the evening memorable for her husband. *Dinner, candlelight, soft music, romance.*

Rifling through her brown bag lunch, Maggie sat at her desk daydreaming about their special night ahead. She realized that there would be a window of time that she and Matt could be alone together in their new home. *Alone.* Her heart pounded in her chest, nervous like a newlywed.

Andrew had an away basketball game and would not need picked up from school until about 8pm. While Abigail had her weekly dance classes, ballet, tap, and lyrical from 5:30pm-8:30pm.

Both children were so full of talent and life. Maggie was thankful they were able to continue their activities while at the Chrysalis Center. She believed that area of stability really helped the children cope with the stress of shelter living and kept them in touch with the childhood they once had before the foreclosure.

She would always be particularly grateful to a family who came forward anonymously and paid Abigail's tuition when rumor of their plight spread through Arlene's dance school. At first, the generous act stung Matt's pride, but he decided to accept the offer when he saw how happy his sweet girl was to stay enrolled in her lessons.

Though Matt kept his raw emotions hidden for the most part, Maggie knew he suffered much pain with the job loss and foreclosure. But through it all, he kept his vision of their family alive. His perseverance and relentless determination to put them on solid ground again made her love him in a whole new way. She had always respected him, but it was different now. There was an admiration and deeper sense of trust that emerged from this season. She was happier now more than ever. *Tomorrow night would need to be special,* she schemed. *Very special.*

Mmmmmmm. Rebecca woke to the smell of bacon cooking. Still half asleep, she laid in bed expecting to hear her mother call out, "Becca! Breakfast!" She rolled over twice before remembering her whereabouts.

Anna's guest bedroom was a true reflection of Anna herself. The room was beautiful, welcoming, comforting and warm; layered with exquisite details. The old-fashioned wallpaper with its tiny rosebud print was the perfect back drop for the antiques and lace curtains. Extravagant crystal lamps adorned both nightstands while humble handmade quilts kept her cozy in the cherry wood queen sized poster bed.

Rebecca had become quite fond of Anna. She knew God put Anna in her life to lead her to Him. *"Thank you, Father,"* she prayed in a soft voice as she reached both arms over head waking up her body with a huge, long stretch. Feeling rested and ready for the day, she bolstered herself out of bed, slipped on a white terry cloth robe from a hook behind the door, and headed downstairs excited to join sweet Anna.

"Good morning!" Anna greeted her guest.

"Good morning!" Rebecca replied.

"How are you?" she asked. "Coffee?"

"Oh, yes. Please."

Anna pulled out a chair gesturing for Rebecca to sit down then poured her coffee into a cup already set at the table. "Cream or sugar?"

"Both, actually."

Anna slid the delicate china server with a matching creamer and sugar bowl toward Rebecca, "Here you go." She then walked across the room to the stove and returned to the kitchen table with two plates of piping hot food.

"Wow!" Rebecca exclaimed. "You shouldn't have gone to so much trouble."

"No trouble at all." Anna explained. "So how was your sleep?"

"Wonderful! Thank you so much."

The women ate for a few minutes in silence then Anna noticed Rebecca's eyes were beginning to fill with tears. "What is wrong, dear?"

"Nothing," Rebecca mumbled with her head dropped.

"Tell me what is troubling you."

"I am embarrassed."

"Do not be embarrassed around me. What is wrong?" Anna pushed for her to confide.

"I wanted a drink last night," Rebecca confessed. "Before you called me to come to dinner, I was really struggling with wanting a drink. Badly."

Anna got up and went to Rebecca's side of the table, bent down and gave her a long hug. With her right hand remaining on Rebecca's shoulder, Anna taught, "You know, Rebecca, your addiction to alcohol is what the Bible calls a stronghold. Meaning it has a strong hold on you. In 2 Corinthians 10:3-5, the Bible says, *"For though we walk in the flesh, we do not war after the flesh: For the weapons of our warfare are not carnal, but mighty through God to the pulling down of strong holds; Casting down imaginations, and every high thing that exalteth itself against the knowledge of God."*

Anna returned to her seat across from Rebecca. "You see, sometimes God delivers us from our strongholds instantly and removes all the fleshly desires associated with that stronghold. And sometimes God delivers us moment by moment keeping us dependant on Him."

"I think He chose moment by moment for me!" Rebecca acknowledged with a nervous laugh.

Anna continued, "When we accept Jesus, we are forgiven and made free from sin, however, we are not free from the human consequences of that sin. The consequence in your life is a physical dependency and an addiction to the drug of alcohol."

"What do I do?" Rebecca asked.

"In Philippians 2:12, the Bible says, '*Wherefore, my beloved, as ye have always obeyed, not as in my presence only, but now much more in my absence, work out your own salvation with fear and trembling.*'"

"Work out? I thought I was already saved?" Rebecca shook her head bemused at this new information.

"You *are* saved," Anna confirmed. "Work out means to grow and change to become like Jesus. The desire to become like Jesus is the evidence of your salvation. The Holy Spirit gives you the power to make the changes."

Rebecca sat quietly taking in all Anna could share.

"Once we are saved, God calls us righteous, meaning we are in right standing with Him." Anna paused and took a sip of coffee, giving Rebecca a moment to absorb the lesson.

"God now sees us through His son. Therefore, He sees us perfect, sinless, completely forgiven. In fact, He sees us just as if we have never sinned. This spiritual condition of a Christian is called justification."

Rebecca nodded her head and folded her arms across her chest. She remained silent and serious, deep in concentration as she brought her right hand up to her chin.

Anna leaned forward across the kitchen table. "As born again believers, we have a personal relationship with God. Sin will still hinder that relationship. But now we can go directly to God, ask Him to forgive our sin, turn from that sin, and then our relationship with God is restored."

"The Holy Spirit will reveal areas of sin in our life where we need to confess and repent. While we pursue growing in God's love, we will become more like Jesus. And the more we become like Jesus, the more free from sin we will be."

Anna continued. "Rebecca, this process of change is called sanctification. It is an individual journey, sometimes called our Christian walk. It is what is meant by..... 'to work out your own salvation...'"

Rebecca beamed with understanding. "I think I get it! We do not work *for* our salvation, but we work *out* our salvation."

"Yes," Anna said.

"So every time I crave a drink, and I cry out to God for His help, and I choose *not* to drink, *THEN* I am working out my salvation," Rebecca stated.

"Yes, Rebecca, that is correct. And now that you know what you are going through, be comforted that the Lord is with you." Anna smiled and reached for Rebecca's hands across the table. "And so am I, dear. So am I."

27

"One more week," Dr. Aru told Bonnie after he examined her this morning on his rounds. "If all goes well, one more week and then you can be released to go home."

Those words rang bittersweet for Bonnie. Sure, she wanted to return home. But she did not want to return to her old life. Too much anger, sadness, frustration and disappointment. She shuttered at the memory of her typical day at work. The walk from the elevator to her corner office was filled with cold shoulders and icy stares. Stress, pressure, more stress then the escape of lonely lunches spent behind her pulled shades and closed office door. *NO!*

"No!" Bonnie shouted out loud pushing herself up to a sitting position in her hospital bed. "NO!" The heart monitor started beeping rapidly triggering a piercing alarm following by Nurse Kelly storming through the door. Behind Nurse Kelly rushed in Anna who had been on her way in for a visit.

The women found Bonnie thrashing beneath the bed sheets, short of breath, tears streaming down her cheeks. As Nurse Kelly silenced the alarm and checked Bonnie's vitals, Anna stood near the door ready to minister to her friend in need.

Nurse Kelly noticed that her patient was visibly calmer at the sight of her visitor. "Come on in," she motioned to Anna to move closer. "Normally, I would ask for the room to be cleared, but Bonnie seems to be responding well to your being here."

"Anna," Bonnie acknowledged weakly after exerting so much energy in her momentary outburst.

"Bonnie," Anna parroted back with a smile and stepped to her bedside opposite the equipment.

Nurse Kelly gave Bonnie a small cup of water. "Take a sip, slowly."

Bonnie nodded her head and obeyed without objection. "Thank you," she said.

Then Nurse Kelly turned the monitors back on and chided, "That was enough excitement for the day. Now take it easy. You understand?"

"Yes, ma'am." Bonnie answered.

After Nurse Kelly left the room, Anna reached in over the bedrails and hugged Bonnie as tightly and as long as she could in that position. "Oh, Bonnie," Anna said as she released her embrace and took a seat in the adjacent chair. "Let's talk." Anna suggested sliding her palm underneath a bar to hold Bonnie's hand and offer assurance.

"Anna, Dr. Aru told me that I will be going home in a week." Bonnie shared. "I am scared."

Anna patted Bonnie's hand and nodded for her to continue.

"I know God loves me," Bonnie shared. "For He saved me physically *and* spiritually."

She paused to slow her breath, then, "But I still feel the same emotionally. I haven't changed a bit. I am still anxious and my thoughts keep racing through all the pain and grief and sorrow. "

Anna scooted her chair in closer to the bed and then tightened her grip on Bonnie's hand for both encouragement and emphasis of what she was about to explain. "The reason you feel the way you do is because you think the way you do. In other words, your thoughts control your feelings. And up until now, your thoughts have been formed by the culture and system of the world we live in."

"What do I need to do?" Bonnie agonized. "Tell me, Anna."

"Renew your mind." Anna answered plainly.

"Renew my *mind*?" Bonnie asked, making sure she heard Anna correct.

"Yes, Bonnie. The Bible says in Romans 12:2, "And be not conformed to this world, but be ye transformed by the renewing of your mind, that ye may prove what is that good, and acceptable, and perfect will of God."

Curious and hopeful, Bonnie asked, "How do I do that?"

"By replacing your thoughts with God's words," Anna described.

"Oh- ok," Bonnie agreed hesitantly.

"Let me help you get started," Anna began. "Tell me a reoccurring thought and the emotional pain it causes you."

"Oh, there are so many." Bonnie shook her head.

"Start with naming one," Anna nudged.

"I think about living alone and I feel depressed."

Anna nodded and waited to see if Bonnie would reveal more to her.

"I think about my job and I feel stressed."

Again, Anna nodded then cajoled, "What other thoughts?"

Finally, the wall broke. Through clenched teeth, Bonnie erupted spewing, "I think about my mother dying and I feel angry."

Then Bonnie's head dropped and her voice turned to just above a whisper, "I think about my body and feel shame."

"Bonnie, listen. Look up at me." Anna paused for eye contact then continued, "Each time one of these thoughts come to your mind, repeat a scripture that is a contradiction to that thought. The most effective expression would be to say the scripture aloud. That is what Jesus did when Satan visited Him in the wilderness. You see, Satan is real and still exists today. He was once one of God's angels. But then he desired to be higher than God. This evil desire caused him to fall and thus become the archenemy of God and his people from that point on. He schemes to keep people from believing in Jesus as Savior. Even after we are saved, he continues his mission by trying to block our growth and thus hindering our ability to lead others to Jesus. He does this primarily by attacking our minds. He knows if he can control our thoughts, he can control our lives. In the desert, when Satan spoke lies to Jesus. Jesus spoke the Word. When Satan spoke more lies to Jesus. Jesus spoke the Word."

"What did Satan do?"

"He left. Along with his lies. Jesus is our example. Follow him," Anna instructed. "When a negative thought enters your mind, quickly replace that thought with a contradicting scripture."

"But, Anna, I do not know many scriptures. Not *any* really," Bonnie sulked.

With a warm smile on her face, Anna reached into her tote and pulled out a pink gift bag stuffed with white tissue paper. "For you, my sister," she said handing Bonnie the present.

Bonnie accepted the gift and reached inside the beautiful shiny bag. When she saw the soft leather bound book, she slowly ran her fingers over the title printed in gold lettering, Holy Bible. She looked up at Anna, "Thank you. Thank you."

"You are so welcome," Anna said. "Now *feed* your spirit. Study the scriptures and deposit the words in your heart. Set aside time every day to read. I believe mornings are best. Start each new day with the Lord."

Bonnie sat leafing through the pages. *No sweeter sound,* Anna thought.

"I recommend you start in the New Testament first. Read through the Gospels which are the Books of Matthew, Mark, Luke and John. In them, you will get to read about the life of Jesus from His birth to His resurrection. After that, I would encourage you to start from the beginning and read straight through from Genesis through Revelation. Read daily as the Holy Spirit directs you. Never read past your level of comprehension. It is not how much you read, but how much you understand. Read a passage and then pause to meditate on it by mulling it over in your mind. Ask the Holy Spirit to speak to your heart about how that particular scripture applies to your life and your individual calling."

"I will do it," Bonnie proclaimed. "I certainly will."

"I am so glad. You see, studying your Bible is never a waste of time. In fact, no matter what you are going through in life, the Word of God is the key to your victory. In Isaiah 55:11, the Lord tells us through His prophet Isaiah that His word will always produce the results that He intends for it to produce. He says, *'So shall my word be that goeth forth out of my mouth: it shall not return unto me void, but it shall accomplish that which I please, and it shall prosper in the thing whereto I sent it.'"*

Anna smiled as she watched Bonnie flip to the table of contents and pull her index finger down the center of the page as if on a search for valuable treasure. "Be diligent and faithful in reading your Bible. God's word is a seed when planted in the soil of your heart will produce good fruit. Out of that fruit, you will in turn sow into the lives of others spreading seed and cultivating God's garden of goodness."

"I am so excited to get started!" Bonnie shared.

Anna stood and started to pace at the foot of Bonnie's bed. "Now, let's get back to how to defeat those negative thoughts still rolling in your head. Remember I told you that Jesus stopped Satan and his lies by quoting scripture?"

"Yes," Bonnie nodded showing agreement.

"Well, we should do the same. Turn to the back of your Bible to a section called the concordance."

Bonnie followed Anna's direction like a good student. "Ok. I see it."

"There is a concordance in most Bibles. It is an alphabetical list of words under which is listed a group of scriptures that contain that particular word in them," Anna defined.

"Hmmmm," Bonnie said as she contemplated the usefulness of this tool.

"There are many ways and many reasons to use the concordance. Today, I will show you one study technique," Anna explained. "This technique will help renew your mind by replacing your negative thinking and its subsequent emotions with God's word." Anna paused and turned to face Bonnie straight on at the foot of her bed, "Like we talked about earlier this morning when we discussed Romans 12:2."

"Yes. Yes, I remember," Bonnie nodded, confirming her recognition of the teaching. "Please. Show me how to study. I am ready."

"Great," Anna said as she resumed her pacing. "To start, think of a word and then find it in the concordance. Next, turn to the scripture referenced and read it."

"Ok."

"From there, I recommend reading the entire chapter that the scripture is located in. This helps put that passage in its proper context. You may even want to read the chapter before and the chapter after to gain an even clearer meaning."

"Alright."

"Now, memorize that scripture. Read it silently, read it aloud, write it down. Sing it! Use whatever method works for you to memorize. Then draw it from memory as you need it to cast down negative thoughts."

"Will you help me with one?" Bonnie asked.

"Sure," Anna agreed. "You mentioned feeling depressed when you think about living alone."

"Yes."

"What is the opposite of depressed?" Anna asked.

"Happiness or joy?"

"Good. Let's look up the word joy in the concordance," Anna instructed.

"WOW! God has a lot to say about joy!"

"He sure does! And now you have a resource to turn to when you feel depressed. Look up and read these scriptures one by one. Listen for God to speak to your heart. Which one is most relevant to you personally?" Anna asked rhetorically then continued teaching. "The Bible is called the *living* word because as you learn these scriptures, they become active and alive in your life changing you from the inside out."

"This is so amazing! So wonderful!"

"May I suggest a scripture?"

"Please."

"Nehemiah 8:10 ....*for the joy of the Lord is your strength.*"

"I love that one. Let me find it," Bonnie said eagerly turning the pages to the book of Nehemiah.

"When I memorize a scripture, I like to personalize it. For example, I would remember Nehemiah 8:10 like this... 'for the joy of the Lord is *my* strength.' Oh, that just builds my spirit so!" Anna practically shouted.

Bonnie repeated with a broad smile on her face, "'for the joy of the Lord is *my* strength!'"

"That's right!" Anna clapped her hands together applauding Bonnie's understanding. "The Word of God is food for your spirit. Feed your spirit and as soon as a negative thought creeps in your mind, draw from your reservoir of God's word. Run it through your mind, say it aloud, write it, sing it, live it! Watch! Mind renewed, life transformed."

"How miraculous!"

"I also like to pray the word. Kind of like praying to God in his very own language, that He created." Anna's enthusiasm was building such a hunger in Bonnie.

"Tell me more," Bonnie asked.

"Loneliness. You mentioned being lonely, is that right?" Anna asked for clarification.

"Yes," Bonnie admitted. "I often feel alone, and lonely."

"Turn to Deuteronomy, the fifth book of the Bible. Read Deuteronomy 31:8, *'And the Lord, he it is that doth go before thee; he will be with thee, he will not fail thee, neither forsake thee: fear not, neither be dismayed.'*" From that scripture, you learn about God's character. That He goes before you, and that He will be with you and not leave you. And that there is no reason to fear or be dismayed."

"Yes."

"So you can pray the Word something like this. *"Dear God, I thank you for going before me. I thank you for being with me always. I thank you for never leaving me, ever. Because of your constant and everlasting presence, I will not fear or be dismayed. In Jesus' name, Amen."*

"Oh, Anna. That is so comforting."

"You see, Bonnie, the Bible is a never ending book of love filled with promises and instruction. Not only does God want you to believe *in* Him. He wants you to believe *Him;* meaning believe Him at His Word."

"Anna, thank you so much for taking the time to teach me these things," Bonnie said shaking her head in sheer amazement. "I will start right now. "...for the joy of the Lord is my strength!'"

"Yes, Bonnie.   '...for the joy of the Lord is your strength'…..and it certainly is mine!"

28

Click. As Maggie turned the key to their new home, she froze momentarily in disbelief. Then without warning, her knees buckled out from under her causing Maggie to nearly collapse onto the veranda. She struggled to reach a nearby stone ledge to steady her shaking body and reel in her emotions.

The relief she was experiencing was indescribable, overwhelming. Had the stress of their homelessness been the adrenaline that kept her going all this time? She began to take in long, deep breaths until her mind cleared and her vision came back into focus. When she felt the strength in her legs return, she pushed herself off the ledge and back to an upright position.

Ready. She lifted her head, pulled her shoulders back, and confidently turned the knob to the front door.

Once inside her heart leaped with excitement. It was hard to imagine that the interior was even more impressive than the exterior of the custom two story. In the massive foyer where she stood, hung the most elegant crystal chandelier Maggie had ever seen. White textured floor to ceiling columns framed the entrance area while the walls were done in a golden faux paint that gave the appearance of actual marble. A sight to behold.

Before going any further, she stepped back outside briefly and brought in two suitcases from off the front doorstep. She set them both down gently on the oriental rug that was centered in the foyer, then instinctively removed her shoes not wanting to mar the polished hard wood floors beneath.

The ceilings were at least fourteen feet high, she figured as she set out to explore the unfamiliar surroundings. Her eyes darted from one exquisite detail to the next. Room by room, she leisurely made her way through the four bedroom floor plan. At last, she finished up in the kitchen, a seemingly central point of the house. There, Maggie's attention was drawn to a magnificent fruit basket sitting on the breakfast bar. The basket was beautiful, wrapped in clear cellophane and tied with a purple satin bow. She carefully opened the small card attached. It read,

"Welcome home Tuckers!

From Craven Residential Communities."

Maggie smiled from ear to ear. She was so proud of her husband. And so glad that he was working for such a caring organization. This opportunity exceeded anything they ever imagined. *Anything. Ever.*

Next to the basket, Maggie spotted a note, hand written on a piece of embossed company letterhead stationary. She read it silently. *"Dear Mr. and Mrs. Tucker, We hope you find your new home comfortable. Please do not hesitate to contact the human resource office if you have any questions or concerns. The utilities will be left on until the end of the month to allow you time to have them transferred into your name. Also, the rental furniture is yours to use until the lease expires at the end of June. If you prefer to move in your own furnishings sooner, please let us know and we will make the arrangements. We wish you many happy memories here at River Ranch."* Simply stunned, she shook her head back and forth in amazement. Utilities *and* furniture! Now those were perks she definitely did not count on! Still dizzy from taking it all in, she headed for the garage through the laundry room to retrieve the groceries from her car that she picked up at the Kroger on the way. To save time, Maggie was determined to make just one trip to the garage. When she opened her trunk, she used both hands to loop through every last plastic bag, stubbornly overloading herself. Her walk back to the kitchen resembled more of a skip. *Happy people skip*, she thought merrily.

While Maggie put away the groceries, she continued to marvel at the beauty of their new home. Not only did she love the design, she loved the location. 7000 Miami River Boulevard. The perfect address for their busy lifestyle. The River Ranch Community was situated on fourteen acres along the Miami River, known for its beautiful views and breathtaking sunsets. Their home was adjacent to the sales office, allowing Matt to keep a close eye on the project's hub 24/7. It was also in walking distance to the swimming pool and playground which she knew would thrill Abigail and Andrew. Maggie was particularly pleased to find out that the school bus would pick up the children right at the guard gate for a mere ten minute ride to their neighborhood school, which just so happened to be the same elementary school they had attended since kindergarten.

On top of everything else, the commute to her job in downtown Dayton was shorter now; just less than fifteen minutes, making it possible for her to pop home and join Matt for lunch on occasion.

Maggie worked hard organizing the pantry and refrigerator, careful to keep out the ingredients for the evening meal. With Abigail and Andrew at their activities until 8pm, she had a special night planned for her husband. For dinner, she would make homemade lasagna, Matt's very favorite dish. She envisioned them dining by candlelight, soft music in the background, maybe even a slow dance before dessert. Romance was foremost on her mind. Matt's mind too, she suspected, so long since they were alone together.

After preparing the casserole, Maggie slid the pan into the oven to bake for forty five minutes, providing her the time to get herself ready for Matt's arrival home at 5pm. With just two hours remaining, Maggie scooted off to the bedroom, wheeling her luggage behind her. The master suite was luxurious with a designated sitting area, oversized his and her walk in closets, and of course, a private bathroom. *First things first*, Maggie smirked. She opened one of her suitcases and dug to find the cream colored lace nightgown that Matt found so appealing. Methodically, she laid the lingerie across the bed and smoothed out the wrinkles.

Glancing at the alarm clock on the nightstand, she hurried into the bathroom and began unpacking her toiletries. As soon as she ran across her bubble bath, she stopped unpacking and started to fill the roman garden tub with warm water, adding in the fragrant liquid until an excess of white foam covered the surface. When the water reached close to the rim, she turned off the faucets and stepped in, one foot at a time. She sunk down deep past her shoulders and rested her head on the back edge of the tub, bubbles surrounding her neckline. Closing her eyes, she pictured how she would greet Matt at the front door. *A loving smile, a warm embrace. Gentle kisses, long kisses.*

That afternoon, Maggie felt like the happiest woman alive. Satisfied, that all she ever dreamed of, came true. Content, that all she ever wanted, she had. A devoted husband and remarkable children. A rewarding job and beautiful home. Good health and good friends. *What more could there be in life?* She thought. *What more could there even be?*

29

Matt could not remember a time he did not love Maggie. It was as if, time before her, did not even exist. He knew this was not the case, for he had the scars to disprove otherwise. Scars from his childhood, both physical and emotional. But, they all seemed to disappear when he met his true love.

Her name then was Margaret Rukovoski. Just nineteen years old, she was fresh from the coal country of West Virginia, when Matt crossed paths with her at Macon paper. She was the cute receptionist. He was the awkward salesman trying to push his way past her to see the company's purchasing agent. His charming ways did not land him an account, but it did land him a date. Fifteen years later, he held no regrets from that sales call.

Matt glanced down at the time on the bottom right corner of his screen. 5pm. *Yes!* He wasted no time shutting down his computer and closing up for the day. He would have to leave a few loose ends until morning, which was a bit unusual for him. However, today was different. Tonight was different. Special. His sweetheart was waiting for him in their new home.

After bidding a good night to his staff, Matt yanked his winter jacket off the coat rack and hurried out the side door with his jacket still in hand. His employees were somewhat puzzled at his obvious rush, but asked not questions; only returned his good night with a polite wave or nod. As the door to the sales trailer shut behind him, a gust of cold air came around the corner, reminding him to put on his coat before he started home.

Matt kept up a brisk pace while he watched the sun begin its descent over the Miami River. The clear sky made the mix of colors that much more brilliant. Matt admired Mr. Craven for selecting such an ideal piece of land to build on. Actually, Charles Craven was considered a visionary in his field. His trademark was creating extraordinary places to live without disturbing nature, but by strategically using the environment itself as his palate. River Ranch was no exception to his reputation.

As he walked along, Matt pushed his right hand into his pant pocket to check on the box. When he felt the crushed velvet, he curled his fingers around the box tightly as if to pass his love on to the inanimate object inside.

Dusk came early this time of year causing the porch light to turn on as Matt neared his front door. His heartbeat quickened as he thought about how he would greet Maggie. *A smile, a warm embrace. Gentle kisses, long kisses.*

Just as he turned the key in the lock, he felt the tug on the door from the inside. The door opened and there before him stood the most beautiful woman. "Welcome home, my love!" Maggie said with a smile, in a sweet, soft voice.

Matt crossed the threshold and without shutting the door, took his wife into his arms. They held each other tight and close, unaffected by the bitter cold making its way indoors. After a long embrace, Matt pulled back and gazed lovingly at his wife. Then he moved the wisps of hair from her brow before taking her face in his hands. Looking deep into her eyes, he said, "Maggie, you are the love of my life. Thank you for marrying me. And for believing in us."

"Matt, you are the love of *my* life. I will always believe in us," Maggie assured him as she tilted her head and closed her eyes, picturing the scene from her afternoon daydream.

Taking his time, he leaned down and kissed her, gently and tenderly. At that moment, a strong gust of wind brushed by them as if applauding their romance. They could not help but giggle at their determination to keep their lips together while Matt almost lost balance using his foot to kick close the front door. A quick hop and his fall averted.

Maggie broke the kiss first, "It feels so good to laugh!"

"It sure does, Maggie Mae," Matt agreed, flirting with her middle name.

"Let's eat!" she suggested, taking hold of his hand to lead the way.

Classical instrumental music played softly throughout the house as the couple walked hand in hand to the dining room. As they turned the corner across from the formal living room, Matt could see the candlelight dancing from behind the archway.

Maggie entered first and stood gracefully beside one of the chairs. Matt did not follow her, but remained motionless in the doorway. The joy on Matt's face spoke for itself, making

163

Maggie so glad she put her full effort into this evening. Matt praised God in his heart, pressed to give thanks before entering the room. His misty eyes drowning from the banquet he saw before him. It was not the unquestionable presentation that moved him as much as the love it represented. His wife's love and God's love. He knew God to be sovereign and that this precious night was orchestrated by Him, for His glory.

"*O, Lord*," he closed his eyes and prayed silently. "*Thank you for bringing us to this moment. Thank you for the time of testing and that you were there with us through it all. You are a good and gracious Father. In Jesus' name. Amen.*"

Maggie interrupted the silence. "Matt," she called out. "Matt!" "Please, come and sit down, honey."

Matt opened his eyes and walked in. Slowly, he circled the table admiring all the effort Maggie put in to making the evening so perfect. The table was draped with a simple white linen tablecloth complete with matching napkins folded into triangles and perched on top of the dinner plates. The place settings were fine china, solid ivory trimmed in a thin gold ban. The flickering, burgundy pillar candles picked up the burgundy tones in the drapes and artwork. Crystal candleholders and glassware offset the centerpiece, a tall crystal vase filled with six red roses, tiny baby breaths and assorted greenery. The silverware balanced out the look, tying in the silver casserole dishes and serving trays.

"Maggie, the table is beautiful," Matt said.

"Thank you."

"And so are you."

Maggie blushed and smiled shyly, acknowledging the compliment.

Matt came around and pulled out Maggie's chair as she took her seat. He paused to massage the tops of her shoulders wanting to show his appreciation for her.

Dinner took almost a full hour as they enjoyed the delicious food and sweet conversation. Following dessert, they moved their date to the living room where the light from the fireplace seemed to lure them in, a touch Maggie planned for earlier that day. They curled up together on the sectional sofa, where Maggie nestled her head on Matt's chest. *Finally home.*

Matt felt the time was right to present Maggie with the box. He slowly pulled it from his pocket and placed it in her hand, "For you," Matt said.

Surprised, Maggie asked, "What is this?"

"Open it!" Matt insisted, sounding like a toddler with a handmade craft to give.

Her eyes popped open wide. "Oh, Matt. It is beautiful!"

Matt chose a charm to go on the gold chain she wore around her neck, the same chain he gave her when they first started dating.

"It is a butterfly." Matt said. "From a chrysalis, comes a butterfly."

"*Chrysalis.* Like the Chrysalis Center we stayed,"

"Yes."

"How beautiful!"

"That is you, Maggie Mae! Beautiful, strong, ready to fly!"

"Thank you Matt!" She unhooked her chain and slipped it though the notch on the charm. Matt slid her mid-length hair to the side, latched the necklace and then kissed her on the neck.

"I love you Maggie Mae. I love you!"

30

Five days had passed without a word since Jake was served the divorce papers, or supposed to have been served. Emma had not heard from Jake, or her attorney. Curious, she put a call into Ken Cross to find out the status. She had an unexpected mixed reaction to not hearing from Jake. Relieved for her baby's sake, but somewhere deep down she thought maybe, just maybe Jake had changed during their separation. That they might be reunited and be a family.

Reconciliation was just a fleeting thought and a dangerous one at that actually. Without evidence of a change in Jake, she knew divorce was her only option. But, it hurt all the same. She began to rock herself back and forth while holding her growing tummy. Admittedly, if only to herself, she was lonely. She wanted to share this pregnancy experience with a husband, like she always dreamed. A loving, gentle, caring husband.

But she didn't get that. The sooner she really, really understood that as a fact, the easier she could move on in life. Looking back, there were signs during their courtship. Signs she dismissed, hoping her love was enough to fix things. To fix him. She married him, despite the warnings, against her instinct. Jake was on his best behavior on their wedding day. But after they were married, things got worse.

The cycles became predictable. Jake would become agitated, sometimes at her, often just at anything or anyone. Then he would fight, verbally at first, insults, name calling. Then, he would be remorseful, extremely remorseful, gifts, flowers, even vacations. Emma would be so depressed after his tirades and be so vulnerable that she welcomed the make up stage, even longed for that time, needing love so badly after the verbal jabs and punches. The cycles became more frequent and started to become physical. First destroying objects, throwing and smashing family pictures, pouring water on them. Taking her clothes out of her closets and throwing them on the floor, pouring water on them. Drowning her possessions, and drowning her soul.

The abandonment was the worst. One especially angry morning, Jake cut the electric cords off the back of the television set and took all the phones from the house. Then as he left for work, Emma watched him leave from the window of their second story apartment. He popped open the hood of her Buick Regal and fiddled with some part. Later, she discovered her car would not start. Emma was all alone, stranded, trapped and scared.

Then there was Bert, their new puppy. Jake was a business owner who ran his company, much like his home. One very bad day, he forced an employee to come to their home and take their puppy and tie it out back of his shop until Emma would apologize to him. Not knowing if Bert had food or water, she groveled and begged for forgiveness. This humiliation just drove Emma deeper into depression. And the more depressed she became, the more love she needed. And Jake was there.

If she had not become pregnant, she did not know if she would have had the courage to leave. The baby was her strength. During another one of Jake's early morning rampages, he sat straight up in bed and threw a dish across the room. No apparent reason. Emma woke to the crash and saw the broken glass scattered all over the clean hard wood floors. For a souvenir of his anger, Emma picked up a chunk of the periwinkle blue glass as a sort of keepsake to remember the danger. The jagged piece has remained in the pocket of the winter coat she wore the day she left him, a tangible reminder to never go back.

There was no time and no room for self-pity. The baby would be here soon. She had to be ready, body, mind and soul. Four months until she would be a mother. May was the perfect month to give birth, Emma thought. Birds singing, flowers blooming, green grass and plenty of sunshine. Her favorite time of year. Yes. Spring was the season for new life. And that is just what Emma needed, *a new life.*

Rebecca had a good weekend, her first sober weekend in a very long time. Even when she went home for the Christmas break, she drank daily. She had heard vodka was the drink that was undetectable. And she heard correct. No odor, no problem, or so she thought. Her parents did not seem to notice her quick and sudden trips to her bedroom throughout the day and night. She was careful not to drink too much at a time hoping to avoid any spikes in her behavior and tip off her family.

At first, she felt somewhat proud of her disguise, like she possessed a special talent for keeping a secret. But before long, a deep, gnawing feeling crowded that pride. For each time she opened her dresser drawer to take out the bottle, she felt sick to her stomach. Not from the liquor, but from the guilt.

Seemingly, she had the anecdote. Her guilty conscience could be quenched with a good, long swig. As the clear liquid rolled across her tongue and down the back of her throat, she could feel her body grow warm all over, from her chest, to her limbs, to her mind. The guilt stopped. Her conscience silenced. Ironic, she thought how the cause of her guilt also took it away.

But after seven days of sobriety, her mind was already becoming clearer. She was remembering things better, she felt stronger and happier. Mostly, she felt thankful for being rescued from the endless cycle of guilt, then numbness, guilt, then numbness. From a pit, to the throne with one decision. A pit of despair to the throne of God. She was still astounded that God loved her personally so much that He made a way for her to trade her sin for His righteousness. There was no value she could ever place on that exchange. Salvation was priceless. Her life before Jesus was such a complete and utter mess. He truly saved her in every essence of the word. Jesus did for her what she could never have done in her own strength. She loved Jesus. She *loved* Him for loving her. Jesus paid a great price for her forgiveness. She was determined not to take her freedom for granted by living worthy of His sacrifice.

Yesterday was the first time she had attended church since surrendering her life to Christ. She met Anna at her home where they drove together to Dayton Community Church on Valley Road near Beavercreek. Although Rebecca had attended church regularly with her family growing up, this Sunday was different. Rebecca was different.

Side by side, they walked into the building. Two friendly folks with nametags greeted them just inside the front doors. Rebecca shook their hands and accepted the bulletin they gave her. At this point, she dropped back a few steps so Anna could take the lead. A mix of apprehension and excitement were all rolled into one emotion as she entered the main sanctuary.

The room was alive. People of all ages filled the large modern space. They were moving in and out of the rows, down the aisles, talking, hugging, and even laughing. The background music added yet more life to the already exuberant atmosphere. Not the traditional environment Rebecca was accustomed to in a church, but she liked it.

Anna chose their seat. Second row from the front, right hand side. Several ladies came over to see Anna and meet her guest. Before she knew it, Rebecca was rushed with women from practically all sides.

"Welcome. Welcome!"

"Glad to have you!"

"Good to meet you!"

They took turns shaking her hands, hugging her, rubbing her arms, stroking her back. She felt their love, their acceptance. *Family.* She was beginning to understand what Anna meant by having a new family. This is Anna's family, her church family. *How awesome!* Rebecca shouted inside.

The lights dimmed suddenly signaling the start of service. The room grew quiet as the congregation returned to their seats. Most remained standing as lights came up on the front platform. Singers, keyboard, drums, guitars, and even a violin. She could not believe her eyes, let alone her ears. When the music started, people sang out loud and clapped to the beat. Yes, clapped. *How fun!* She did not hesitate, but enthusiastically joined in the celebration. The lyrics were scrolling on large screens to the side of the stage making it easier for Rebecca to follow along.

The next song slowed down the pace. She watched as people around her closed their eyes, swayed their bodies, and raised their hands. Some raised one, some both. *How beautiful!* She surrendered herself to the song and lifted her hands too. Unsure of the posture at first, she pushed past her pride to engage fully in the experience around her.

The refrain of the song repeated many times allowing Rebecca to learn the words and close her eyes. The band leader paused to pray mid-song encouraging the people to press in as they worshipped. The song picked back up again. Rebecca was not certain what 'press in' meant, but she decided to sing the words directly to Jesus. She pictured Him in her mind. There was a park, bright green grass, beautiful shade trees, a blue sky and plenty of sunshine. She saw the resurrected Jesus, dressed in white, sitting on a bench. She took the seat next to Him and looked into His face, so bright she could not make out the details. He placed His arms around her and held her. *Father and friend.* Then she pulled back to look into His eyes, but Jesus would not let go of her. He took her hands. She felt the nail scars in His palms. Scars for her.

As she sang the words to Him, she was no longer cognizant of herself, her problems, or anything really. She just saw Him and His light. Tears rolled down her cheeks. She could feel them soaking her face. But she would not stop worshipping. Her heart seemed to have cracked open and His light was pouring in. His love flooding her body and soul. His Spirit filling her spirit. Healing her every wound. Mending her every hurt. She knew. She knew in that moment, however brief, their spirits joined as one. His Spirit, the Holy Spirit communicated to her spirit. A divine communication. A transfer of love, unconditional and everlasting.

She heard talking. The Pastor was praying for God to stir the hearts of the people in the church and in the city. Rebecca opened her eyes and slowly brought her attention back to the service. When the sermon began, she listened closely to the message, looking up scriptures, taking notes. But her mind kept drifting back to worship.

She saw Him. She experienced Him. She knew she would never be the same. *Never.*

Mean. Pure and simple. Bonnie knew why she had not heard from any of her co-workers. She had been mean to them. Day in and day out, just plain mean. So when Henry poked his head through the door of her hospital room that Monday afternoon, she was more than surprised.

"May I come in, Bonnie?" he asked sheepishly while tapping on the half open door with the back of his knuckle.

Bonnie was in the middle of lunch when her visitor arrived so she quickly swallowed her bite and laid down her utensils. "Sure thing. Come in!"

She wiped her hands and mouth with the linen napkin, then moved her tray off to the left hand side of her bed. After pushing herself up straighter in bed, she smoothed her hair down and put on a smile, the only grooming that she could think of in time. She was not expecting company. And certainly not Henry Spone.

"I am sorry to interrupt your lunch. I can come back?" he offered.

"You are not interrupting. I was just finishing. Please, come in," she urged, not wanting him to leave.

174

Henry carried in an extravagant arrangement, a contemporary square pewter vase filled with wild orchids of varying sizes and colors. Bonnie was taken aback. *What a day! A visitor and flowers!*

"How are you?" he inquired as he timidly approached her bedside.

"Much better. Thanks."

"For you," he said while lifting up the orchids.

"They are absolutely beautiful. Thank you so much."

"Should I set them here?" he asked, indicating the table across the room.

"Perfect."

Bonnie began to wonder why Henry was there. She really did not know him that well. Or at all, for that matter. He was head of the IT department at Hanson, Bradford and Skeen. They had worked together for years. But outside of regular business, they had never shared more than a few words. *So why visit her?* She had always thought Henry to be a nice guy. Intelligent, polite and reserved. But past that, she never gave him any mind. Until today.

Today, he was handsome. Something was different. Like she was seeing him for the first time. His boyish hair cut, his friendly smile, his gentle eyes. Everything about him seemed new to her. Though Bonnie knew that she was the one brand new. That God had given her a new set of eyes, along with her new heart. She was attracted to goodness now. And Henry was a good man.

He was a good man all along, she figured. But she was blind to the potential of relationships before she knew Jesus. Filled with Christ's love now, she was ready. To make friends, reach out to people, tell her story, and maybe even fall in love.

Henry and Bonnie talked for hours. Simple chit-chat to deep pontificating. Her life was taking a new direction, unfolding in an unexpected way. There was no mystery. The Lord set the stage. He was the director. It was the second act. She would play her part. Listen and obey. Listen closely and obey.

31

Cocoa and cookies. After the lesson tonight, Anna planned to ask her students to join her in the den for cocoa and cookies. She thought the women would be apt to linger longer with the record cold temperatures they were experiencing this winter in Dayton. Most winters in western Ohio were mild, but this year was the exception. More snow fall than years past, and definitely more ice. Though Anna enjoyed the serene beauty of winter with its snow covered landscape and ice draped trees, she did not enjoy the traveling challenges that accompanied the season. With temperatures hovering in the teens of late, just a small amount of precipitation in the air would turn the roads into a sheet of ice, often unnoticed by hurried drivers. Salt trucks were a regular sight in town, trying to keep up with the constant change in weather conditions.

Anna wanted to make the evening special tonight. For starters, she would bake a dozen or so cookies from scratch. *Chocolate chip*, she decided, always a favorite and besides she knew the recipe by heart. Anna loved everything about baking, from the feel of dough in her hands to the first sample out of the oven. But mostly, she loved gifting her treats. Even when times were tough, and money was scarce, she could still be a giver. Sugar, flour, butter, eggs, never seemed in short supply. When Samuel was alive, every Friday, she would pack him enough homemade sugar cookies in his lunch pail to share with his whole crew. She smiled thinking about how happy that ritual made her husband. Tonight, she would create that happiness here, in their home. *Oh, how Samuel would have liked that idea!* Anna felt energized remembering him and his love.

And she needed that energy, for there was much to do before her guests arrived. Dusting, vacuuming, mopping, and the like. These preparations were not chores to Anna. Rather they were acts of love. Rebecca, Emma, Maggie, and Bonnie. The women God placed in her life to love. He was providential, orchestrating and overseeing, leading and guiding. She was the vessel He was using to reach them. Her role was to sow. Not sew, but *sow* into their lives. Sow God's love and God's word, and God's plan of salvation.

Anna's quiet time this morning was powerful. Though she has walked with the Lord for many years now, there were days they seemed closer, more intimate. Today was definitely one of them. Her practice was to read five full chapters daily. One in the Old Testament, two in the New Testament, one in Psalms and one in Proverbs. She liked to keep her reading plan flexible, disciplined, but not too rigid. Some days she may read more, some days less. Regardless of the number of chapters per day, she always seemed to read through the whole Bible each year, finishing up around Christmas Day.

Her appetite for the Word was as ferocious as ever, insatiable at times. Admittedly, she was dependant, and glad to be. For without Jesus, she would wither. Weak? Yes! But isn't everyone, really? Only she knew where to turn. And now so did Rebecca and Bonnie. Her heart still heavy for Emma and Maggie, praying God would give her boldness to share the Gospel with them, and that their hearts would be open to receive the good news.

As she read this morning, the word *refuge* kept coming to mind, interrupting and breaking her focus. *Refuge. Refuge?* She would loose her place and begin again, reading slower and more intensely the second time. Again, *refuge.* But when she turned to her chapter in Psalms, she knew. God was getting her attention, speaking to her, preparing her for something. He was about to confirm in his Word what He had already spoken to her heart. *"The Lord is our refuge and strength, a very present help in trouble." Psalm 46:1* She did not understand yet completely, but she knew to get ready.

Her kiss goodbye was longer than usual. As much as Matt missed Maggie on Monday nights, he knew how much she enjoyed her sewing class. And the evening out was good for Maggie. Good for Matt too, as it gave him a chance to spend one on one time with Abigail and Andrew. He got the children's dinner, checked their homework, and tucked them into bed. All the things Maggie did regularly.

Matt had always loved his family. Yet ever since he recommitted his life to Christ, he had a deeper appreciation for them. It was as if he now looked at life and love with a new set of eyes. He desired to be more engaged in their lives on every level. He cared about their needs. Not just the obvious ones like food and shelter, but the details that before seemed insignificant, if he noticed them at all. He treasured their uniqueness. Now, he was drawn to serving them. Not out of obligation, but out of a love that he really never knew. Now that he was connected again to God through Jesus, he was tapped into the source of love and he could not wait to love more and more.

Six o'clock. Anna was touching up her lipstick in the hall mirror when she heard the clock chime six. Carefully, she returned the cap on her favorite shade and dropped the tube into her purse hanging on the coat rack around the corner. She hurried toward the foyer where she took one last look around before deciding to open the front door and brave the elements. With only a small shawl wrapped around her thin frame, Anna found the cold to be harsher than she expected. The blast whirled around her body, stinging her face and seeping into her bones. Her eyes watered and nose ran almost immediately. She huffed into the air to see her breath, fascinated like a child to watch as the vapor cloud vanished before her eyes. Though only outdoors a few minutes, her toes were already growing numb.

She stomped her feet hard several times and began to pace in order to circulate her blood.

Then she saw them. Anna quickly forgot any discomfort when she spotted Rebecca, Emma, and Maggie. *They are here!*

"Come in!" she hollered out, happy they arrived at nearly the same time. "Watch your step."

She stepped back inside her house and held open the front door wide to welcome them into the warmth. The three heeded Anna's advice and cautiously walked up the stairs and filed into the foyer, one by one. They took turns greeting each other with smiles and hugs as they took off their coats and boots.

"Hey Emma!" Rebecca said. "How are you?"

"I am good. How are you?" Emma returned.

"I have been doing great. Thank you," Rebecca answered then turned to Maggie. "How are you?"

"I am good, too. Glad to be here," Maggie said.

"Well, I am glad you are all here," Anna shared. "Hopefully Bonnie will join us next week. She is supposed to be discharged this Thursday."

"Praise God!" Rebecca said.

Emma and Maggie looked at Rebecca quizzically and then exchanged glances with each other wondering what came over their fellow student.

Anna recognized the awkward stare and changed the subject before Emma and Maggie had the chance to put Rebecca on the spot about her comment. She knew Rebecca could not help but talk about her new love. For Jesus' love was greater than any crush, date, boyfriend or even husband. Rebecca was gushing. It was natural for a new believer to be so in love that they tell everyone and anyone. Anna knew it was real and beautiful and pleased the Lord. But Emma and Maggie would not understand. Not yet.

The women followed Anna into the sewing room where they retrieved their projects from the designated storage area. There were two waist high oak shelving units along the left hand wall, positioned side by side to look like one large piece of furniture. Each student was assigned their own individual shelf, complete with plastic tubs of assorted sizes to help keep their projects neat and organized.

Last week, Rebecca had finished pinning her pattern to her material and was ready tonight to cut out the various parts to her tote bag. Maggie was at the next step. Her placemats were going to be double sided, formal and elegant on one side, every day contemporary on the reverse. Having already cut out the material during the previous class, tonight Maggie was going to pin the two sides together, carefully folding and tucking the edges inside to create a smooth finished hem around each mat. Emma was closest to finishing her project. She had sewn together the two sides of her baby blanket last week. Tonight she planned to border the blanket with a satin trim to add beauty, as well as keep the edges from fraying apart. Bonnie's comforter project understandably had a long way to go until completion.

During the last class she attended several weeks ago, she was able to lay out her material and start pinning the sides together, inside out at this phase, before sewing, reversing, and stuffing. Anna hoped for Bonnie's return next week, when she could pick up where she left off prior to her hospital stay.

Anna spent time individually with each of the women, guiding them along the way. While she moved from student to student, she would pause to examine their work and offer instruction. First, she stopped and adjusted Rebecca's grip on her scissors, showing her an easier and better way to cut fabric. "Try this," Anna suggested.

Rebecca tried the new hand position on her own. "Wow! That makes a big difference. Thank you."

"You are so welcome. Keep up the good work!" Anna encouraged.

Next, Anna moved on to help Maggie pin her placemats, preparing them to be sewn together the following class. Since this step can be tricky, Anna demonstrated the technique to her. She showed her how to tuck the edges inward, and then press down and hold each section firmly with the left hand, while pinning it in place with the right hand. "Go slow, Maggie. Better to take longer and be precise," Anna advised.

"I will," Maggie committed. "Thank you for your help."

After watching Rebecca and Maggie work for a while, she walked over to assist Emma. She gently tapped Emma on the shoulder and smiled, "May I?"

"Please," Emma replied, sliding her chair over a smidge to the left.

Anna leaned over Emma's right shoulder to help her start pinning the satin trim around the border of her baby blanket. But as Anna began to fold the piping along the edges, she noticed that sections of the hem were crooked; the stitches weaved in and out of the one inch margin. Though only slightly off, Anna advised Emma to hold off attaching the trim for the night. Instead, she recommended tearing out portions of last week's work, just the areas that were more or less than the one inch mark. Anna showed her how to remove the unwanted stitches one by one using a seam ripper, a handy tool which typically did the job without harming the fabric. After that, Emma could then start over and redo the areas missing stitches. She would need to pin those areas flat first to keep the material from bunching up. Then she would be ready to sew, careful the second time to run the material through the machine perfectly straight at exactly the one inch mark. Anna knew the process would be time consuming, but Emma would be grateful later with the results of her extra effort.

Emma looked discouraged at the work ahead of her and the delay in completing her blanket. Reading her expression, Anna set out to encourage her with some wisdom. "There is a life lesson here. Not just for Emma, but for all you ladies. When you have made a mistake, stop. Go back to where you went out of line, remove the unwanted area, and redo the right way. Then remember what you learned to avoid repeating that same way. The second time, after guidance, is always better!"

Anna smiled, satisfied with her instruction and the women's progress. Their projects were all at different stages, much like the women themselves. Starting out, starting over, on hold, or winding down. Actually, Anna thought, sewing was symmetry for living life. The journey is a spiritual one, whether realized or not. God is the designer and we are his creation. Jesus is the pattern; the Holy Spirit is the teacher. The Holy Spirit cuts us into the shape of Jesus, and God loves us through the whole process.

After an hour or so of sewing, the ladies closed up their projects and moved to the den for cookies, cocoa, and conversation. Light hearted talk, giggles, and laughs. The evening ended with hugs all around.

"Good night ladies! See you next Monday. Drive safe. The roads could be icy."

"Ma'am?" The elderly man asked while knocking on the driver's side window. "Ma'am?"

When there was no response, he knocked harder on the fogged up window and raised his voice, "MA'AM?" Still no response.

Sensing the urgency, he tried the handle. Upon finding the door unlocked, he quickly opened it in hopes the woman inside would hear him better and respond to his call. "Ma'am? Can you hear me?"

He knew better than to move an accident victim, more likely getting that information from a TV show than any real emergency training. Instead, he took off his coat and laid it carefully across her body for extra warmth. Then he called 911.

"Yes. There has been a car wreck."

Pause.

"On South St. Clair Street. Near the intersection of South St. Clair Street and East Third Street. The car hit a tree in front of the entrance to Cooper Park."

Pause.

"Come quickly. Please. There is a woman injured. She is unconscious."

Pause.

"Yes. I will stay with her. Thank you."

Maggie could hear everything, but she could not speak. Her mind worked, but she could not engage her mouth to move. Or any other part of her body for that matter. It was like her mind and body was no longer connected. She strained to lift her head, to sit up, but nothing happened.

Maggie was scared. *Why can't I move? I need to get to Matt. And Abigail and Andrew.*

She recalled taking a left onto South St. Clair Street. She must have taken the turn too fast because when her car hit a patch of ice, she lost control of the vehicle. The car went into a tail spin before slamming headfirst into a tree. The air bag deployed instantly. The impact knocked her unconscious until she heard the stranger come to her aid and rescue.

The sirens were getting closer. Maggie knew the ambulance would be there any minute to take her to the nearest hospital. She hoped that someone would call Matt. As she left the sewing class, she called him to tell him she was on the way home. His number would be the last call placed on her cell phone before the accident.

The sirens stopped. The sound of commands and directives filled her head.

"Let's go!"

"Hurry!"

"Bring that over here!"

"Quickly!"

That was the last she remembered before she slipped away.

It was eleven o'clock and there was still no sign of Maggie. Matt tried calling her several times, but kept getting her voicemail. Something was wrong, Matt knew. While pacing the floor of their living room, Matt decided to call Dayton General.

"Emergency Room. What is your emergency?"

"I wanted to see if my wife had been taken there tonight?" Matt grew tense.

"What is her name, sir?"

"Maggie Tucker."

Matt could hear the keys clicking on the computer, as the nurse searched her records.

"I have a Margaret Tucker?"

"That must be her. What happened?"

"Sir. I cannot give you anymore information over the telephone."

"Oh, no. Please," Matt begged.

"I am sorry. But, sir?" she rebutted.

"Yes?" he replied.

"Come down to the hospital. Quickly!"

"I am on my way!"

Matt wasted no time. He ran to the refrigerator and located the magnet with an advertisement for Yellow Taxi.

"Yes. It is an emergency. Can you pick me up and take me to Dayton General? I am at 7000 River Ranch Boulevard. I will be waiting at the main entrance. Yes. Thank you."

Matt rushed into the children's bedroom carrying in their shoes. He flipped on the overhead light and tossed their shoes onto the bed.

"Hurry! Please get your shoes on and come with me."

"DAD!!"

"What is going on?"

"There is no time for questions. I will explain on the way. Grab your coats. Let's go! We are meeting a cab at the front entrance."

The sleepy children obeyed their father, shoved on their shoes and followed Matt out the front door. All three jogged to the main entrance to the community, icy air blowing through their clothing.

"Oh, God," Matt prayed. *"Save her! Save her!"*

32

She could recognize him anywhere, even from behind. It had been over five months since she last saw Jake, but Emma could not mistake the blue work pants and leather Bengal's jacket. His hair was longer than usual, lying just over top of his collar, but those silky curls definitely belonged to her soon to be ex-husband. She always loved his locks. But *so* did the others. Women fondle his locks like they would a new born baby. *Oh, how beautiful*, they would say and right in front of her. *Oh, how gorgeous.* The nerve! Yep, that was Jake, alright.

Emma watched him from across the store as he stood staring into the beer cooler. Her heart pounded in her chest, her legs trembled beneath her. *What should I do?* She needed gas. The needle was on red. Normally, she would not have come inside to pay, but today, of all days, her debit card failed at the pump. Without options, she quickly handed the clerk her card, never taking her eyes off Jake. "Five dollars pump twelve," she said just above a whisper. She could fill up later, now she had to escape. *Hurry,* she said under her breath. *HURRY!*

It was 6:30am Tuesday morning. Emma's shift at the hotel began at 7:00am, another good reason to hurry. Meanwhile, Jake had opened the beer cooler and leaned in to grab his usual beverage. She figured he was still up from the night, and then

Emma remembered his old familiar saying, "It is lunchtime somewhere."

With a six pack in hand, he turned and looked down the aisle, allowing the cooler door to shut on its own. That was the moment Emma's world stopped. As if in slow motion, a petite, young girl came right up alongside Jake and slid her arm up and under that over worn, outdated, lint magnet of a jacket. Then so natural, so familiar, Jake turned toward blondie and kissed her, and nuzzled her nose. She could not hear their words, but she clearly heard the giggle and coos.

Bile came up in her throat. She was going to be either sick, or faint. Or both. The clerk waived Emma's card toward her line of sight to get her attention, but she did not respond.

"Miss," the clerk gently addressed her.

"Miss," he repeated and tried clearing his throat.

"MISS!"

Emma jerked, snatched her card, and bolted out the front door. She raced to her car, holding her bulging belly with one hand and wiping her tears with the other. The next five minutes were a blur as she went through the motions of filling her tank and speeding away.

But she did not get far. Two blocks from the convenient store, Emma pulled off the side of the road, unable to drive in her state of mind. When she did not hear from Jake after he was served the divorce papers, she suspected he had moved on. But actually seeing Jake with another woman brought her to a completely new place of brokenness. A place she did not know how to return from on her own. *Why couldn't he love me? What was wrong with me? What is better about her?*

In the midst of her sorrow, a sudden and sharp pain formed in and around her abdomen. She buckled over laying her forehead on the top of the steering wheel. *NO! Not my baby!* When the pain came again, and stronger, she knew she was in trouble. Reaching for her purse, she found her cell phone in the side pocket and pushed 911.

"Help!" she panted. "I need help. I am in a red Buick Regal, on Toledo Road, just a couple blocks north of the Quik Stop. Come quick, please." She could not fight any longer. The darkness closed in. Her body fell across the front seat, slumped over the armrest, still and cold.

———————

He could not get her out of his mind. Unable to stop replaying the events of last evening, sleep failed him miserably. At 7am, Thomas gave up trying, rolled out of bed and headed to the kitchenette for a strong cup of coffee. Rolling out of bed was no longer a figure of speech for the seventy two year old, but a literal description of his wake up style.

Not knowing how long he would be in the area, Thomas rented a room by the week at a motel close to downtown. The accommodations were modest, yet clean and comfortable complete with a telephone, coffee maker, and cable television.

After opening the drapes to let some daylight into the room, Thomas took a seat at the small dining table next to the window. He sipped on his coffee while leafing through a Gideon Bible he pulled from the nightstand drawer. It had been a long time since he read God's Word. *Too long*, he decided. The hard cover book was stiff from not being of much use lately. Thomas chuckled to himself thinking how the condition of the book also described his own condition these days.

Thumbing through the book of Proverbs, he came across what seemed a fitting scripture for his journey. *"A man's heart deviseth his way: but the Lord directeth his steps."* Proverbs 16:9

Sure, Thomas devised a way. He had come to Dayton, Ohio with a plan, a perfectly made plan. But God must have had another route for him to take, or at least a temporary detour.

The detour included a stop by Dayton General Hospital to check on the injured woman from the car wreck last night. Never had he been the first on the scene of an accident and the experience left him quite shaken. After a short visit, Thomas then would resume his original plans for the day.

After all, he had tracked her down this far. He had to find her, before it was too late.

———————————

When Anna woke up at 8am Tuesday morning, she felt an urgent need to pray. Without questioning her instincts, she slipped out of bed and fell straight to her knees. She placed her elbows on the bed, closed her eyes and bowed her head, resting her forehead on top of her interlaced fingers.

"Lord, thank you for prompting me to pray. I believe someone I know is in trouble. I sense the need to intercede on their behalf. Bring them safety, protection, health and healing. Restore them body and soul. If they do not know Jesus as Lord and Savior, may today be the day of their salvation. Thank you for hearing and answering my prayer. In Jesus' name, Amen."

She continued to stay on her knees for several minutes, soaking in the Lord's presence, gathering the strength she needed for the day ahead. *"I love you, Lord,"* she prayed softly aloud, longing to linger, and remain close. In the eyes of her heart, she envisioned the Lord in all His glory, as a golden, radiant light, wrapping His arms around her and lifting her tall and strong. *"Thank you, Lord,"* she continued, confident of His omnipresence, thankful for His everlasting love.

Suddenly, the telephone rang. Anna opened her eyes and glanced over at the nightstand. *Who could it be so early?* She got up off her knees and headed for the telephone.

"Hello."

"Yes."

Pause.

"Yes."

Pause.

"I will be right there."

195

———————————

Rebecca was in history class when she heard her cell phone vibrate inside her book bag.

She knew she should wait until after class to check her phone, but she felt pressed to look right away. Oh, how she loved her new relationship with Jesus. Rebecca knew the pressure she was experiencing was actually the Holy Spirit, the third person of the trinity, prompting her into action.

As quiet as possible, she slid her hand down into her book bag and riffled around until she found her phone. Anna had called twice. There was also a new voice mail. She glanced at the wall clock. It was 9am. Class was not over until 10am.

She could not wait. She *would* not wait. *Something was wrong.* Gathering her things, Rebecca shoved them in her bag, and headed for the door of the classroom. She nodded her head toward the professor and mouthed a humble apology before her exit.

Anna was there for me. I will be there for her. Always.

33

The waiting room of the Intensive Care Unit was full, packed with tired, weary faces exhausted by worry and fear. There were no empty chairs but for the one located behind a small desk in the front corner of the room. A hospital volunteer would normally be stationed there to monitor the visiting hours and rules. This morning; however, there must have been a staffing issue as the desk was temporarily unmanned. Instead, at the top of each hour, a nurse would enter the room and deliver the following instructions. "You have thirty minutes. Starting now. Family only." Then, she would prop the door wide open with her back as the visitors lined up and filed past her and in through the double doors to the secured area.

Matt was pacing the floor when Anna arrived. Although they had never met each other in person, Anna had a strong hunch she spotted him in the back of the room. She saw a tall, thin man, in about his middle forties, walking back and forth, with his head hung low and both hands plunged deep into his pockets. He never looked up, never even glanced her way, as if staring at his shoes would somehow keep him in control. Yet the most telling sign of recognition was the two adorable children behind him, sound asleep, arms and legs intertwined as they shared a tiny, most uncomfortable looking couch.

"Matt?" Anna inquired.

Without saying a word, Matt turned and walked slowly toward Anna, forcing a faint smile.

"Thank you for coming down," he said, choking back tears.

Anna stood on her tip toes and gave him a great big grandma hug. "How is Maggie?" she asked.

"She made it through the night," he reported. "The doctors said that is a good sign."

"Indeed, that is a good sign," she agreed. "Would you like to go in to see her now?"

"I just missed the 10am visiting time. I will have to wait until the next one at 11am."

Andrew and Abigail began to stir, hearing the voice of their father. "Dad?" Andrew woke up questioning. "How's mom?"

"She is going to be fine," Matt answered.

Andrew and Abigail sat up at the same time, both squinting as they adjusted their eyes to the light. They looked at Anna, then back at their father.

"Andrew. Abigail." Matt began. "This is Anna. Your mother's sewing teacher."

"And friend," Anna added with a smile. "Nice to meet you."

Matt squatted down in front of the children and put one hand on each of their knees for reassurance. "I asked Anna to come down to sit with you while I go in to visit with your mom."

"How did you find her?" Abigail asked, always a stickler for the details.

"The blue index card on the fridge at home," Matt explained. "It was the ad for your mom's sewing class which contained Anna's contact information. I grabbed it and stuck it in my pocket last night as we left to catch the taxi cab to the hospital. I thought it might be helpful."

"I remember the card, Dad," Abigail said, seemingly satisfied with her father's answer.

"Well, I am glad you called me," Anna assured them. "I will help your family any way I can."

"Thank you," Matt replied quietly, his lack of sleep starting to show.

"Would you like me to take the children for a walk? Maybe go to the cafeteria for some juice or a donut?" she suggested so Matt could have some private time.

"Uh," Matt stammered, hesitating at first. He knew the children needed a break, but at the same time he did not want to let them out of his sight. For the children's sake, he agreed. "Ok. Sure."

While still in the squatting position, Matt stretched out his arms to scoop up and love on his children. Abigail and Andrew stood and jumped into their daddy's arms. They held each other tight for several minutes, exchanging hugs and kisses, relishing the affection more than ever.

Matt watched as the door shut behind them. His stomach was in knots. He had to be strong for his children, but inside he ached. A deep, intense ache, as if he was already experiencing the unmentionable loss. *I can't lose her*, Matt thought.

Please God, heal my wife, he pleaded under his breath. *Please.* Matt realized his prayer sounded more like begging rather than a son confidently approaching his loving father. *Lord, why am I so fearful? Why am I struggling with disbelief? Help me to overcome my doubt. O God, remove this feeling of dread and terror. Fill me with your Holy Spirit, again and again. Fill me to overflowing. Replace worry with peace. Replace fear with faith. Replace anger with forgiveness. Replace doubt with trust. Replace sin with love. Thank you, my Lord.*

Bonnie had an 11am follow up appointment at Dayton General. Although it had been less than a week since her release, the doctors wanted to be sure she was responding well on her own. Fortunately, she had another week of sick leave available and would not need to return to work until the following Monday.

The hospital appeared to be especially busy when Bonnie arrived. Unable to find a parking spot in the designated outpatient area, she decided to splurge the five dollars for valet service.

She drove through the roundabout stopping in front of the valet stand which to Bonnie's surprise was surrounded by a half a dozen or so of shivering, scowling people. When the valet employee came jogging back to his post, the crowd seemed to press in even further coveting to be the next patron selected. Bonnie found the scene quite enlightening, even amusing a bit. Sure, the weather was blistery, but now that she has chosen to slow down and not do life in a hurry, she could see the wasteful and detrimental effects of rushing. She empathized with their plight. Before her heart attack, Bonnie would speed through the day, piling more and more on to her plate. And the more on her plate meant the more on her *plate*. Kitchen plate! The combination ended her up here at Dayton General Hospital.

But, the combination also led her to the Lord. A destination for which she would be forever grateful she arrived. She thought back how God tried to get her attention for so many years, in so many ways. He never stopped pursuing her. The heart attack, the interruption, simply gave her pause to listen.

Bonnie put her car into park and took her place in line with the other red cheeked, watery eyed individuals. She prayed silently while she waited her turn. *Oh, Lord, thank you for saving me. Thank you for restoring my health and giving me new life. Thank you for Anna, your daughter and faithful servant, the willing vessel who carried your message of salvation to me. Bless her for being obedient to your command to go and preach the gospel. May the seed Anna sowed into my life grow strong that I may now be used by you. For you. In Jesus' name, Amen.*

"Next," the young uniformed fellow spoke to Bonnie.

"Thank you," she replied as she handed her car keys over to the valet worker. "Thank you very much."

Bonnie tucked her claim ticket into her wallet, and then glanced at her watch to check the time before heading into the main lobby of the hospital. Dr. Aru was located on the third floor of the Becker Cardiac Wing. She planned to take the elevator to three and follow the sky walk over to his office. After pushing the up button, she stood patiently staring overhead at the floor numbers, counting them down as they lit up one at a time. While she was waiting, she thought she heard her name.

"Bonnie?" the voice called in the distance.

Me? Are they calling me? She wondered, curious some, but not enough to turn and investigate. She kept her eyes on the declining numbers, while still listening for the sound of her name again.

"Bonnie?"

There it was again.

Then came the tap on her shoulder.

———————

"No."

"*Please, ma'am.*"

"No. I am sorry, sir," she repeated. "I cannot release any information unless you are family."

"But.... but....," Thomas persisted, attempting to give a reason for an exception.

"I *am* truly sorry," she insisted and then pressed a button on her headset to answer a telephone call, or at least to pretend to answer anyway.

"I understand," he replied, reluctantly.

A line was beginning to form behind him at the registrar's desk, so Thomas decided to step aside and recalculate his plans for the day. He certainly respected the receptionist's work ethic, but her adherence to hospital policy was making it difficult for him to find her. In the condition Thomas found her in last night, he was convinced the woman would have been admitted as an overnight patient. In fact, by the looks of her injuries, he suspected she would be an in patient for a number of days, if not longer.

After lingering momentarily near the registration desk, Thomas milled about the lobby repetitively, wearing an imaginary pattern into the tile. When his legs grew weary, he headed toward a small cluster of chairs by the main entrance to sit and rest for awhile. The intermittent bursts of cold air from the automatic doors refreshed him, even though they were mixed with exhaust fumes from the idling cars in the valet line.

He dropped his head back against the chair and closed his eyes for a minute to collect his thoughts. But with cell phones ringing, and people yakking all around him, Thomas could not relax. He had to find the woman from last night. Once he knew she was recovering well, he would be able to concentrate on the reason he came to Dayton.

Determined to resolve the problem, Thomas sat up in his seat and looked around the lobby, hoping to come up with a new idea. The clock on the wall read 10:50am. He was behind schedule for the day. But then again, he was behind schedule, period. Behind by years, actually. Had he just known sooner, things could have been different. *Oh, how I should have been there for her?* He vowed to make it up to her.

34

"She is seven months along."

Anna heard a nurse shout as she watched a stretcher speed down the hall past her and the children. She took her right arm and pressed Abigail and Andrew into the wall to keep them from getting run over by the rescue team.

No? Anna questioned herself. *It couldn't be?*

She thought the young lady that rolled by was Emma. *What a resemblance?* But with the oxygen mask over the woman's face, it was hard to know for sure. Yet something inside Anna stirred, gnawing at her to follow behind.

"Abigail. Andrew," she addressed the children in a serious tone.

They looked up at her with sullen, tired eyes.

"Before we head to the cafeteria, I need to check on something first. Actually, check on some*one* first," she explained.

"Sure," Andrew agreed. "I am not hungry anyway."

"Me, neither," Abigail chimed in.

"I am sorry for the delay," Anna apologized.

She took the children by the hand, and hurried down the hall, trying her best to catch up to the stretcher that had whizzed by just moments ago. Her walk turned into a run when she lost sight of the group turning the corner up ahead. *Faster,* she thought. As she and the children quickened their step and made the turn, she was just in time to see the stretcher being pushed through a set of steel double doors.

Maternity Ward. She stopped and read the sign overhead, letting her brain slowly digest the meaning of the words. *Maternity Ward?*

Anna did not hesitate. With Abigail and Andrew at her heels, she marched into the maternity ward, purposeful and single-minded, knowing full well they would be stopped and questioned at any moment. Sure enough, an orderly approached her and the children immediately.

"Hello ma'am," he greeted, standing tall and close.

"Hello sir," Anna returned politely.

"My name is Joseph. How may I help you this morning?" he asked.

"Yes. A woman was just brought in here on a stretcher. By ambulance, I believe."

"Yes ma'am," the man acknowledged.

"I think I know her," Anna said. "I think she is Emma Harper."

The man nodded his head, listening politely, but not confirming or denying the identity of the patient.

"May I see her?" Anna waited, hoping for a positive answer.

"Are you family?" he asked.

"No, sir," she answered truthfully, although Emma felt like a daughter to her.

"Well, then I -- ."

Anna interrupted, "Sir, I am as close to family as she has right now."

"What is your name?" he inquired, with compassion in his eyes.

"Anna Lovett."

"I will go check on her," he said. "And if she is able to have visitors, I will ask her if she would like to see an Anna Lovett."

"That would be wonderful," Anna shared. "Thank you."

"But, the children can not go back," he warned. "I cannot budge on that rule."

"I understand," Anna replied. "I am watching the children while their father visits their mother in ICU."

"I am sorry," he said warmly, sympathizing with her load.

"We will all wait here until you come back with a report," Anna planned.

"Sounds good."

"If I am able to visit her, I will return here after I bring the children back to their father following his 11am visitation."

"Great."

"Please let her know I am on the way."

"Sure will," he promised. "She is blessed to have a friend like you."

"Thank you," Anna smiled.

I am the one blessed. I have so much to be thankful for. I am saved and satisfied. Forgiven and free. Alive and well. I have a

heavenly father, good friends and good health. I am blessed. O,
Lord, thank you. How I am blessed.

"Rebecca!"

"Hey!!!" Rebecca leaned in for a hug. "How are you?"

"I am good," Bonnie said, realizing Rebecca was the voice calling her name. "What brings you here today?"

"Well, I do not know the details, but Anna left a message on my voicemail asking me to come down here. She did not say anything else," Rebecca explained. "I hope everything is alright. I tried calling her back several times, but my call keeps going straight to her voicemail."

"Oh, dear," Bonnie shared with a frightened look in her eyes.

"I am going to try again now," Rebecca said, picking up on Bonnie's concern for their mutual friend.

When the elevator door opened, Bonnie took a step backward and gestured to the others nearby to go on in ahead of her. The passengers piled in close together. The last person in held the door open to check if Bonnie would be boarding.

"I will take the next one," Bonnie told them. "Thank you."

Rebecca stepped away from the elevator doors to place her call to Anna. Bonnie followed.

"Hello Anna?"

"I am here at the Hospital. Where are you? Are you alright?"

"Oh, oh," Rebecca choked up. "I will meet you there."

Rebecca looked at Bonnie with tears in her eyes.

"What is it?" Bonnie asked firmly. "Tell me, please. Is Anna ok?"

"Anna is fine," Rebecca confirmed. "It is Maggie *and* Emma."

"*Both* are here?"

"Yes"

"What happened?"

"Maggie was in a car accident last night after sewing class. She is in ICU," Rebecca reported. "And Emma was brought in by ambulance to the maternity ward. Anna is in the maternity ward now waiting to get a report on Emma. She is also watching Abigail and Andrew while Matt visits with Maggie." Rebecca drew a breath before continuing. "Once Anna gets the status on Emma, she will head back to the ICU waiting room. I will meet her there." Rebecca paused and scrunched her eyebrows while thinking through the sequence. "Then when Matt comes out from his 10am visit with Maggie, and if he is ready to watch the children, then Anna and I will go to see Emma at that time."

"Oh my!" Bonnie clamped a hand over her mouth and closed her eyes tightly as if offering up a prayer.

"Do you want to come?" Rebecca asked.

"I have an 11am doctor appointment," Bonnie explained. "May I meet up with you after that?"

"Most definitely!"

"Rebecca, what is your cell phone number?" Bonnie asked. "I will call you the minute I am available."

"555-4712"

"You better go!" Bonnie egged on.

Rebecca turned and ran down the hall to ICU, weaving and bobbing folks along the way. "Excuse me. Pardon me," she would alternate saying as she passed people by.

"Lord, please be with Maggie and Emma now. Heal them. Restore them. Comfort them. Thank you, Lord. Thank you."

35

When Thomas spotted the sign for the hospital chapel, he saw it as much as a spiritual sign as a directional one. The Lord was indeed calling him to come seek wisdom and counsel. Actually, the Lord called him on a regular basis, and on a regular basis Thomas delayed responding to that call. As if it were yesterday, he could hear Pastor Bob, his childhood preacher, bellow out, "Delayed obedience is disobedience." Well, that sermon sure had his name all over it.

Thomas knew that on his knees is where his problems were really solved. He could not quite pinpoint the reason behind his resistance. Pride, stubbornness, a willful spirit were among the top three. But mostly, Thomas was convinced he could handle things on his own. After all, don't 'they' say, "God helps them who help themselves."

Thomas had come to discover that cliché is no where to be found in the Bible. In fact, the Bible says quite the opposite. *"God is our refuge and strength, an ever present help in trouble." Psalm 46:1.* Pastor Bob explained it like this. We are to ask for God's help in life, acknowledging that we are dependant on Him, and that we need Him as our only source of strength. When God reveals His plan for us, we are to cooperate with corresponding action that lines up with His Word. God gives us room within that plan, a perimeter to move about in. We are to remember that God's plan is always best. Always.

Even when we do not understand or His way does not seem to make sense. Pastor Bob would also point out that we can choose to step outside the perimeter God draws for us. In or out. That choice, that movement is called free will. Our soul consists of our mind, our will, and our emotions. Once we are saved, our souls are made free; therefore our wills are free. Before we are saved, our soul; ergo our wills, are enslaved to sin and we are unable to participate in God's plan. Only through salvation, can we fully reach our *God given* potential.

The subject of free will both baffled and comforted Thomas at the same time. Wouldn't it be simpler if God just *made* us love Him? Just *made* us all be good? He was God, after all. He could do anything, right? These were the questions that nagged at Thomas. But on the other hand, they also brought him solace. God's desire is for all to know Him. He offers His love, manifested in Jesus.

We can choose to accept that love, or not to accept. If we accept, we receive power given by the Holy Spirit to *choose* to make good choices over bad. If we do not accept, we are in bondage to sin; and we do not have access to the power of the Holy Spirit, therefore choices are left up to human strength. In fact, if we do not accept, we are evil, inherently so. Sure, we can intermittently show good outward behavior, but our spirit, our soul, remains evil until regenerated through submission to Jesus. Many are lost today. And many of the saved exercise their free will and choose to step outside the perimeter of God's plan. Thus evil exist in the world.

Almost noon now, Thomas rose and walked slowly toward the chapel. His heart was full of conversation to share with God. *Abba, Father. Teacher, guide. Confidante, friend. Lord, Savior. Now, forever.*

Moments later, Joseph came out and told Anna that Emma was stable for now, but that she had been through a trauma.

Trauma? Anna thought. *What does that mean?*

Joseph also told Anna that Emma had been unconscious since her arrival, but that she momentarily open her eyes his last check on her. She was awake long enough for Joseph to get her permission for Anna to visit.

Anna was relieved Emma agreed and she reaffirmed her plan with the orderly to return in about fifteen minutes after bringing the children back to their dad in the ICU waiting room.

"Thank you, Joseph. You have been very kind," Anna said.

"You're welcome. See you soon." Joseph smiled and turned back to his work.

Matt had a great visit with Maggie. She was alert for the very first time since the accident. Matt wasted no time sharing his love and devotion with her. Then he cut to the chase.

"Maggie, life is short. Sometimes shorter than we planned for. I want to be a good husband."

"You are," she got out.

"Well, I need to talk to you about something very serious. It can't wait."

"You are scaring me. What is it?"

"Eternal life."

"You mean heaven?"

"Well, uh, uh," Matt stuttered, feeling guilty for not sharing sooner. "Well, uh. Heaven *or* hell, actually."

When Maggie didn't respond, Matt pulled his chair in closer to her bedside. He noticed her eyes growing heavy, blinking and straining to keep them open. He shook his wife's arm a bit to get her attention. He empathized with her sleepiness, but he could not wait a second longer. He had to tell her.

"Maggie, I know you are tired. I know you are weak," Matt acknowledged. "But, I must tell you."

"Please, Matt," she whispered. "Tell me."

"Maggie, I could have lost you last night," Matt started. "I am so thankful to be with you right now. I should have told you sooner. The minute I found Him again."

"Found who, Matt?"

"Jesus."

Maggie scrunched her eyebrows together as she tried to piece together what Matt was talking about to her. "I know who

Jesus is," she said with a click of her tongue. "The 'reason for the season' guy, right?"

Matt ignored her hint of sarcasm and pressed on. "I realize you know *of* Him," Matt agreed. "But you need to know Him personally, establish and build a relationship with Him."

He took her hand and continued, direct and relentless, "Maggie, if you would have died in the car accident last night, or if you would die tonight, here in the ICU, would you know for sure that you would go to heaven?"

"Honey," she sweetly addressed him, as she looked into his eyes and smiled lovingly, hoping to settle her husband's nerves. "I am a good person. Of course, I would go to heaven."

His heart was pierced deep as he listened to Maggie's belief. His empathy turned to anger as he thought of all the lost souls that Satan deceived by the 'good person' theology. The lie that blinds, like none other. His own beloved wife, not an exception.

Matt cupped his face into his hands and dropped his head muffling the short small sniffles of this broken man. Broken not from condemnation, but from affirmation. The Holy Spirit had revealed the truth to him. He would be called into account for the spiritual condition of his household. He repented in his heart to the Lord, and then to his wife.

"Maggie, please forgive me. I should have taken better care of you."

"Matt," she interrupted firmly, shaking her head in disagreement. "Stop," she begged as she lifted her hand signaling him to stop the needless and unfounded confession.

"No, Maggie. I will not stop," he said, determined to own responsibility for withholding the truth from his family. "Maggie, I love you so much. My love for you compels me to give you the information that will save your life. You *can* know for *sure* that when you die you will go to heaven and live with God forever and ever. That certainty gives you peace in your heart and purpose for your life."

Maggie made a valiant effort to sit up in bed as she hung on her husband's every word. Approaching her fortieth birthday soon, she had recently been contemplating her life's true purpose. "Matt, I have been thinking about my life lately. I want so much to know my purpose. Why am I here? Why was I even born? And now why was my life spared in the car accident last night?"

"You see, Maggie, once you have this knowledge, not just in your head, but deep down in your heart, your purpose is revealed. Actually, all who have this heart knowledge have the same purpose in life."

"What is it then?" Maggie asked.

"To *say so*," Matt said.

"Huh?" she questioned.

"In Psalms 107:2, the Bible says, 'Let the redeemed of the Lord *say so*.'" Matt recited.

All who have been redeemed are commanded to *say so*, to one another, to the lost so they will be saved, and to the saved so they can be strengthened. God asks us in this passage to share our testimonies of what the precious blood of Jesus accomplishes in our lives. The testimony is not the result of the sacrifice; it is the sacrifice itself and the love that propelled the sacrifice."

"I am still confused," Maggie scrunched her eyebrows.

"You see, if a believer is hungry and their need is met, it is not the provision that is the testimony. The testimony is the blood of Jesus shed for us out of love. That love filled the heart of a believer who provided the food to a hungry neighbor. It always goes back to the blood. It always goes back to Jesus."

"Well, I know Jesus," Maggie boasted as she slid down under her sheets.

"Sweetheart, Jesus is more than a man whose birth we celebrate at Christmas. He is our Savior, the Savior offered to the entire world."

"I know," Maggie acknowledged.

"Maggie, do you really know?" Matt pushed his wife. "See, we cannot save ourselves by being a good person. The only way to be saved is to believe in Jesus. He said in John 14:6, *'I am the way, the truth, and the light. No one comes to the Father except through me.'*"

"Matt, *I* need a Savior."

"Maggie, would you like to pray for this new life? Would you like to pray that God will save you both in this life and the life to come?"

"Yes, Matt."

"The Bible says in Romans 10:9, *'That if thou shalt confess with thy mouth the Lord Jesus, and shalt believe in thine heart that God hath raised him from the dead, thou shalt be saved..'*"

"Do you believe that Jesus is God's son?"

"Yes."

"Do you believe that Jesus died on a cross as a substitute for you, personally?"

"Yes."

"And do you believe that he was buried and was risen from the dead after three days?"

"Yes."

"Maggie, then pray with me now." Matt took her hand. "Repeat after me."

"Dear God," Matt whispered.

"*Dear God,*" Maggie repeated in this same tone and volume.

"I am a sinner," Matt began.

"*I am a sinner,*" Maggie prayed.

"I am sorry for my sins. Forgive me and save me," Matt continued.

Maggie cries, "*I am sorry for my sins. Forgive me and save me.*"

Matt took her hand and nodded his head to encourage her. "I believe that Jesus is your son and that He died on a cross to pay for my sins."

"I believe that Jesus is your son and that He died on a cross to pay for my sins," Maggie repeated slowly and deliberately.

"I believe that Jesus was buried and after three days, He resurrected from the dead," Matt prayed.

"I believe that Jesus was buried and after three days, He resurrected from the dead," she prayed.

"Jesus, I invite you to come into my heart and be my personal Savior and the Lord of my life," Matt said with great excitement, knowing the journey ahead of his dear wife.

Maggie smiled, *"Jesus, I invite you to come into my heart and be my personal Savior and the Lord of my life!"*

"Holy Spirit, baptize me, fill me to overflowing with your power and love," Matt tightened his grip on Maggie's hand.

"Holy Spirit, baptize me, fill me to overflowing with your power and love," Maggie said boldly.

"Father God, I love you and will live every day of my life for you," Matt slid forward in his chair.

"Father God, I love you and will live every day of my life for you," Maggie nodded for confirmation.

"In Jesus' name, Amen," Matt concluded.

"In Jesus' name, Amen," Maggie prayed.

Matt stood up and sat next to Maggie on the bed. He leaned in and hugged her, welcoming her into the Kingdom of God.

They remained in their sweet embrace for several minutes, soaking in their love and the presence of almighty God.

36

Simultaneously as she opened her eyes, hot, burning tears poured down Emma's cheeks. Waking up was no longer an option she wanted to participate in. As the pain grew larger and larger, she desperately desired to go back to where she could not feel the agony of her reality. She was convinced that only sleep, coma, or even death was the only state she could exist in now. For nothing she knew could relieve her of this great and terrible ache.

It was not a physical injury from her collapse that caused her pain. It was the memory which brought her to the collapse that was destructing her from the inside out. Never before had she experienced despair in a way she could not process. The pain was not just in her mind and thoughts, but she felt it physically. Like the pain was a separate, tangible, invasive entity that forcibly took up residency inside her body. The pain had become part of her being that would not leave. She hurt deep, deep inside, like a presence or a filling of sorrow that could not escape. Over and over, she felt surges of pure overwhelming sadness beating her in the depth of her gut, never stopping, never relenting, constantly hollowing out her soul.

I just want to be loved, Emma moaned. She curled into a fetal position to try and grab hold her pain. *Please, love me*, she pled in a whimper. Sure of her need for love, but unsure of who or where the source of that love existed. Emma contemplated pretending she did not see Jake with the other woman. She considered just telling herself that he would return, a good man, to love her and raise their baby. But she knew the denial of reality was the emotional vehicle that drove her to this place of suffering.

The intense episode of remembering and exploring her feelings left her exhausted. Before long, she drifted into a shallow sleep. As her head lay on her tear soaked pillow, she still winced in pain. Even while sleeping, she remained burdened. Short gasps of air followed tormented expressions on her beautiful face. *Love me; love me,* her lips moved. *Love me.*

———————

After Bonnie signed in at the desk, she remained standing at the counter hoping to speak to the receptionist before taking a seat in the waiting room. A few minutes later, the glass window slid open and a woman reached out to retrieve the registration clipboard.

"Excuse me," Bonnie said leaning down into the opening.

"Yes? How may I help you?"

"Do you know how long until I will see my Doctor?" Bonnie inquired. "I just ran into a friend of mine in the lobby. There has been a medical emergency with a mutual friend and I would like to join them after my appointment."

"I understand. Let me check on the wait and I will let you know," the woman offered.

"Thank you."

Bonnie took a seat where she could face the door leading back to the examination rooms. She would be ready the moment she was called back.

And sure enough, seconds later, "Bonnie." A young nurse stood propping open the door and searching the waiting area. "Bonnie?"

Bonnie stood attentive, "Right here!"

"Great!" she said. "Come on back."

"Thank you," Bonnie replied.

"My name is Melinda," the nurse said. "We met in your recovery room, but I was not sure if you remembered me being there."

"I do remember you. Thank you for taking such good care of me," Bonnie shared her gratitude.

"How are you today?" Melinda asked.

"Good, thank you," Bonnie answered.

Bonnie followed Melinda closely down the hall stopping at the scale for a weigh in. She used to dread this part of visits, but now she accepted the challenge and appreciated the accountability.

"Bonnie, you dropped eight pounds since your release from the hospital," Melinda announced enthusiastically. "Good job!"

"Thank you," Bonnie replied humbly.

"Actually, it is more than just the weight loss." Melinda noticed. "You seem like a new person."

"Well, I have been given a second chance in life. Physically, but also spiritually," Bonnie explained her motivation.

"Go on," Melinda urged wanting to know what made Bonnie change.

"I have a new life now," Bonnie stated plainly.

"A new life?" Melinda questioned.

"You see, I know my Creator now," Bonnie leaned in slightly as she began to share. "God made me to glorify Him in all things, and that includes my physical body. I am now motivated to examine what I eat by the love God has for me and I for Him."

"How do you *know* he loves you?" Melinda asked.

"By faith," Bonnie declared.

Melinda look around wondering if any of her colleagues were in earshot of their conversation knowing how religion is often a taboo subject in the workplace. After giving Bonnie a nod and knowing look, she said, "Bonnie, let's get you set up in one of the examination rooms. Follow me."

Bonnie took the clue, stepped off the scale and kept up pace behind her nurse. The women eagerly walked into the room one at a time like 'BFF's" ready to share a new secret. Bonnie hopped up on the exam table while Melinda took a seat in the chair situated catty corner next to the table.

Melinda began, "What do you mean *by faith?*"

"You see, There is one God who exists in three persons. God the Father, God the Son, and God the Holy Spirit," Bonnie started out.

"Kind of like, I am a nurse, mother, and wife?" Melinda sought clarification.

"Yes, that is right," Bonnie confirmed. "You see, God sent his son, Jesus, to earth as a baby born of a virgin."

"Oh, yeah! Christmas! I love that holiday!"

"Well, the love does not stop at His birth," Bonnie explained. "God's love is made personal and real at the cross."

"I know that story too. Easter, right?"

"It is not just a story. It is history. *His* story," Bonnie shared.

Melinda nodded; listening closely to Bonnie's every word.

"We are all sinners and deserving of death. But God made a way for us to have forgiveness of sin and eternal life. Jesus is that way. In fact, He is the *only* way."

"Go on, please,"

"Jesus took our sins and paid our penalty for them when He willingly died on a cross. He took our place. He took the punishment that we deserved. Who else would ever do that for you?"

"No one I know!"

"God does!" Bonnie exclaimed, and then quoted John 3:16. *"For God so loved the world, that He gave His only begotten*

Son, that whosoever believeth in Him shall not perish, but have everlasting life."

"I believe!"

"After Jesus died, he arose again in three days."

"I believe! I believe!!"

The women embraced spontaneously, and then Melinda pulled backed with a puzzled expression on her face. "But what does that all have to do with *how* you have made the changes in your life?"

"I am so glad you asked me how I have changed," Bonnie smiled. "God's love and God's power."

"Please, tell me more."

"Well, I know now that I am God's creation made in His image. Out of love for Him, I respect my body just because He MADE ME!" Bonnie exclaimed. "I have a new life now and I want to live it healthy, happy, and whole."

"I want what you got!" Melinda blurted out.

"You can. Pray with me to receive Jesus' forgiveness and love. Commit your life to Him and be free!" Bonnie shared. "The Bible says in John 8:32 *'And ye shall know the truth, and the truth shall make you free.'"*

Bonnie hopped down off the table and came along side Melinda's chair. She put her left hand on Melinda's back and her right hand on Melinda's shoulder. With closed eyes, Melinda bowed her head and folded her hands as she repeated the prayer that Bonnie led her in. After a few minutes, Melinda looked up with glistening eyes. She stood up and hugged Bonnie.

"Thank you for sharing your story with me," Melinda expressed warmly.

"Thank HIM!" Bonnie acknowledged.

The ladies giggled like school girls experiencing puppy love. But God's love was so much more. Unlike human love, God's love lasts and will endure all time.

37

"Let's go over here for a minute before we see Emma," Anna directed Rebecca as she pointed to a couple of chairs lined up along the wall in the hall just outside the double doors to the maternity unit.

Rebecca followed Anna and took a seat next to her. Anna pulled out her Bible from her oversized purse. She turned quickly to Ephesians 6:13-17 and read aloud, "*Wherefore take unto you the whole armour of God, that ye may be able to withstand in the evil day, and having done all, to stand. Stand therefore, having your loins girt about with truth, and having on the breastplate of righteousness; And your feet shod with the preparation of the gospel of peace; Above all, taking the shield of faith, wherewith ye shall be able to quench all the fiery darts of the wicked. And take the helmet of salvation, and the sword of the Spirit, which is the word of God.*"

Rebecca listened intently while Anna read in her usual sweet, soft voice. When Anna was finished, she took Rebecca's hands in her own. "Rebecca, I sense that Emma has really been wounded, emotionally more than physically. We need to ask the Lord to prepare her heart to receive His love and to prepare *us* to deliver the Good News to her."

"Is that what the scripture you read was talking about?" Rebecca asked.

"Yes, Rebecca," Anna answered. "Emma is dead spiritually, dead in her sins. When God awakens the heart of one of His own, they will be able to hear the Gospel and be able to respond. The scripture I read you is God's instruction for believers to prepare themselves for battle."

"Are we going into *battle* in Emma's room?" Rebecca asked in a strange tone.

"Yes," Anna confirmed. "A spiritual battle."

Then Anna took Rebecca's hands firmly and prayed, *"Heavenly Father, please prepare Rebecca and I to preach the gospel to Emma. Soften Emma's heart. Allow forgiveness to flow through her so that her heart will be fertile soil for which the seed of God's Word will be planted, take root, and grow. Equip her supernaturally to hear the good news and receive the love of Jesus Christ. We trust that you have ordained this moment in time. In Jesus' name, Amen."*

Thomas left the hospital cafeteria and headed back to the main lobby. He was determined to be more direct with the volunteer at the desk this time around. When he made his way to the registration area, he saw a frail, elderly woman already engaged in conversation with the receptionist. He guessed her to be hard of hearing by the way she leaned over the counter and positioned her ear right up close to the desk clerk's mouth. After several minutes, the woman turned to leave, seemingly satisfied with her answer.

"Excuse me, Ma'am." Thomas said to the woman, stopping her before she walked away.

"Yes?" she stopped momentarily and looked his way.

"May I help you with anything?" Thomas asked her while taking a pace backward to allow her more room.

"I am fine, son," she replied. "Thank you for asking."

Thomas watched as she shuffled on, one hand on her walking cane and the other hand pulling behind her portable oxygen canister. Her struggle made him wonder how his own sister was getting along. *Was she in good health? Did she need help? Would she even want his help? When would he find her? Or would he find her at all?*

Thomas recognized his negative thinking and stopped himself before his fretful thoughts carried him too far off from the task at hand. "First things first", he said under his breath as he stepped up to take his turn at the registration desk. Once he knew the woman he found at the accident scene last night was in stable condition, then he could resume the search for his sister.

See, to Thomas, finding his sister was not just a goal, or a dream, or a bucket list wish. Finding his sister was a necessity that would affect their family for generations to come.

The clerk behind the counter cleared her throat to get Thomas' attention. Thomas looked at her with a blank stare as he reeled his thoughts all the way back into the present moment.

"How may I assist you?" asked the friendly lady seated behind the counter wearing a pink and white stripped jacket and huge volunteer button.

"I need to check on the condition of a woman brought in last night who was involved in a car accident," Thomas asked directly.

"Do you know about what time?" she inquired.

"Yes. I know the exact time because I followed behind the ambulance," Thomas replied. "10:42pm." He held his breath and silently prayer for favor.

"Actually, there happened to be a woman admitted at 10:44pm," she shared. "The ambulance picked her up at South St. Clair Street."

"Any other details?" Thomas pushed.

"The paramedic's report says she was alone in the vehicle when they arrived. And that the vehicle had hit a tree at the entrance of Cooper's Park."

She has to be the one, Thomas thought. Then he dared, "May I see her?"

"Maggie Tucker. She is in ICU. First floor, East Wing."

"Thank you! Thank you!" Thomas replied with great gratitude as he practically sprinted toward that very direction.

No hospital policies or government laws can block the Lord's doors. He willed this connection. Thomas knew that truth deep in his spirit. He simply knew.

Abigail and Andrew looked angelic as they slept quietly in ICU waiting room chairs. Their heads leaned into each other's for support as their father's jacket laid over top of them like a cozy, warm blanket. Matt was seated in an adjacent chair, leaning forward with his face buried in his hands, deep in thought and prayer. He could not go in to visit Maggie until Anna or Rebecca returned to look after the children.

Although he was *physically* exhausted from all that had happened in the past twenty four hours, he was *spiritually* recharged. Consumed by God's love, he wanted nothing more but to pour out praises and thanksgiving to Him for saving his wife. *Oh, how their life would change now,* he dreamed. With Jesus Christ at the center of their marriage, all things were possible.

"Thank you, Lord", he prayed just above a whisper. *"Thank you."*

Emma was already awake when Anna and Rebecca entered her room. The curtains were still drawn closed, despite it being the middle of the afternoon. The only light came from a small table lamp next to Emma's bed. Anna resisted the urge to change the atmosphere and decided it best to get close and comfort the sweet girl as quickly as possible.

Although Emma's eyes were wide open, she did not blink or even glance their way as the women approached her bedside. Instead, she laid on her right side perfectly still; staring blankly toward the door. Her position was child like with her knees pulled into her chest and her hands clasped just below her chin.

Rebecca's heart ached as she saw the sadness on Emma's face. She began to doubt if she would be of any help in this situation. Anna sensed Rebecca's fear so she placed a firm hand on the small of Rebecca's back and gave her a tiny nudge to encourage her to be strong and courageous.

"For where two or three are gathered together in my name, there am I in the midst of them," Anna spoke out loudly. "Matthew 18:20."

Rebecca took that profession of scripture as a signal to begin ministering to Emma. She moved in very close, pressing her body into the bedrail. Gently, she worked her left hand in between Emma's interlocked fingers. She then took hold of Emma's hand and gripped it hard, like she was about to pull her up out of a deep ditch. She held on tightly, as if making a silent pact with her friend. With Rebecca's right hand, she stroked Emma's soft, blonde hair, using mostly the tips of her fingernails like a comb.

At the very moment of touch, a single tear, so big, so very big, appeared at the inside corner of Emma's left eye. It slowly spilled out, rolled down the side of her nose, and then down her cheek, before it landed audibly on her pillow. Just one, lone tear.

Anna slid along side Rebecca and bent down giving Emma a kiss on her damp cheek. As she rose from the kiss, she paused at Emma's ear and whispered, "I love you, Emma."

Love. Love? Emma could not remember the last time she heard those words. "I love you, Emma." With those words, the dam broke and Emma's tears began to flow and drench her pillow. Rebecca continued to hold her hand and stroke her hair while Anna massaged her shoulder and upper arm.

After a few minutes, Emma rolled on her back and looked both Anna and Rebecca in the eye one of a time. "Thank you," she managed to squeak out.

"How are you?" Anna asked.

"I am ok," Emma answered in a serious tone. "And the Doctors said my baby is ok too."

"Do you want to talk about what happened?" Rebecca followed up.

"The last thing I remember is driving away from the gas station terribly upset. I had just seen Jake *with a girl* inside the store when I went in to pay," Emma relayed, agitation rising in her voice.

"I am sure that was hard," Anna empathized, nodding her head.

"I can't believe it!" Emma went on. "I mean – I CAN believe it!"

"Well, I guess it will take more than a break up milkshake to get over this!" Rebecca boasted.

Anna and Emma glanced at each other with a puzzled expression and then looked over at Rebecca. "Did you say, *'break up milkshake'*?" Emma asked scrunching her forehead.

"Yep. Ole' family secret for gettin' over a heart ache!" Rebecca confirmed with a bit of a southern twang.

"That's what I thought you said!" Emma smiled and then started to laugh as she half considered giving the idea a try.

Anna and Rebecca joined in the laughter. Soon, the room was full of giggles and snickers. Emma was grateful for the comic relief. She knew the reprieve was but temporary, making her grateful even more.

38

Bonnie pushed L for lobby when she stepped into the elevator. She had just called Rebecca, like she had promised earlier, and made plans to meet up with her at 4pm in the hospital cafeteria. Rebecca was actually in Emma's room when she took Bonnie's phone call. She quickly informed her that both Maggie and Emma were stable, but that she would fill her in on the rest of the details over coffee and perhaps a quick bite to eat. Bonnie agreed and looked forward to being brought up to speed, hoping she could help in some way.

As the doors closed shut, she offered a silent prayer to the Lord for the good health report she received at her doctor's appointment. She truly believed her heart attack was a blessing, a divine interruption in her life. The experience prolonged her *natural* life, and led her to accept the gift of *eternal* life. Her heart was renewed, physically and spiritually.

Now, she desired to be used of God. The dialogue with her nurse minutes ago was just a small taste of what being a vessel for God felt like and Bonnie wanted more. She enjoyed the boldness God gave her to share all she knew about Jesus and salvation. The conversation was comfortable, yet exhilarating. She felt God's power to speak the right words, at the right time. Her confidence in God's love was so real, so genuine that sharing the gospel was a true joy.

What Bonnie lacked in Bible knowledge, she made up for in zeal. Her burning desire to tell others about how the Lord worked in her life inspired her to learn His Word. She would dig in and study it, digest it, and store it in her heart and mind. Then, she would be ready, at His service, waiting for her Father's call.

A far cry from an accountant, Bonnie chuckled, as she thought about all the vast changes in her life. *I guess that is why the Bible says I am born again!*

When Thomas spotted the sign that read ICU waiting room, he quickened his pace anxious to head in and find out about Maggie's condition. He was relieved to be one step closer to putting last night to rest, and moving forward in his search for his sister. Hopefully, he would be heading back to his hotel room this evening for a good night's sleep, before scouring the town tomorrow morning.

Thomas believed that God knows every need and that He is concerned with even the smallest details of a believer's life. The desk clerk giving him Maggie's name and location was the favor of God. Some would contribute God's favor to luck, chance, or coincidence; but Thomas knew to give credit where credit was due.

He also believed that Christ followers should walk in the favor of God regularly, not just now and again. As a parent loves their child and desires the best for their life, so likewise even more does Father God love His children. Thomas prayed that when he found his sister that she would have a strong faith and fervent prayer life. He hoped that they would be able to have spiritual discussions and perhaps take some Jesus journeys together.

Thomas opened the door to the waiting room to discover every chair occupied with tired, weary looking people. He scanned the room to see if he recognized any faces from the scene of the accident. One gentleman did seem vaguely familiar, but Thomas did not want to disturb him, in case he was mistaken. He walked over to a desk near the front corner of the room where an elderly man sat behind, flipping through a magazine. The man wore the identical jacket and identical volunteer button as the lobby desk clerk had worn.

"Excuse me, Robert," Thomas said to volunteer, reading his name badge.

"Yes, sir. How may I help you?" Robert replied.

"Could you show me to the Tucker family?" Thomas asked. "Maggie Tucker's family."

"Oh, yes," Robert agreed as he pointed to Matt, Andrew, and Abigail. "Those three folks, back left corner, starting from the end table and going right. Man in plaid, children sleeping."

"Thank you," Thomas said gratefully.

"Good people," Robert said. "I heard they haven't budged an inch since the 'Mrs.' came in last night."

"Thanks again," Thomas said while nodding to acknowledge Robert's praise.

Thomas slowly made his way to where the Tucker's were sitting. He stopped short so not to startle them, especially the children. Matt noticed Thomas heading his direction and made eye contact as Thomas came closer.

"Mr. Tucker?" Thomas asked to confirm the man's identity.

"Yes," Matt answered.

"I am Thomas Fletcher," he said. "I found your wife last night and wanted to check on how she was doing?"

Matt jumped up. "Oh, Mr. Fletcher," Matt extended his hand exuberantly. "Good to meet you, sir. Thank you so much for attending to my wife. The paramedics said that your quick response was what saved her life!"

"The good Lord saved her life, not me," Thomas credited the maker and giver of life.

Matt's ears perked up when he heard Thomas mention the Lord. *Could the man who found his wife be a brother in Christ?* Just then two seats opened up on the other side of Abigail and Andrew, still fast asleep. Matt motioned toward the chairs and asked, "Would you like to take a seat for a moment?

"Yes," Thomas nodded. "Yes, I would like that very much."

As the men took their seats, Matt blurted out his burning question, "So, are you a believer?"

"For certain!" Thomas beamed. "I take it you are also?"

"Since my youth," Matt shared. "Well, I took a detour; feel asleep at the wheel; lost my way for a bit. But I am back now in right relationship with the Lord. I just recommitted my life recently. And I am so glad I did!"

"Matt, find comfort in John 10:28," Thomas said confidently. *"'And I give unto them eternal life; and they shall never perish, neither shall any pluck them out of my hand.'"*

"Thank you, Mr. Fletcher," Matt said. "I appreciate your reminder. Jesus is speaking to His sheep in that verse, right?"

"Yes. Jesus is speaking to His sheep." Thomas explained. "His sheep are *true* believers. Jesus is saying that nothing or no one can take true believers from Him. He is saying that true believers are to be at peace knowing that their eternal life is an irrevocable promise. Jesus is assuring true believers that they are secure in their salvation."

"God *is* gooood!" Matt rejoiced.

"Amen, brother!" Thomas agreed.

The two sat back at ease, knowing they were family.

"Oh, and please," Thomas paused. "Call me Thomas or brother. *Mr.* Fletcher is for old guys!"

After the brief round of laughs, Anna dove straight into the big conversation and the purpose behind their visit. *Emma's salvation.* She was glad Rebecca agreed to join her on this mission. Anna recalled in the Bible how disciples were sent out two by two to preach the gospel. In pairs, they could support and encourage each other. As partners, they showed unity of beliefs. As she stood next to Rebecca along Emma's bedside, Anna could relate to the need and value of partnership. Following the pattern from scripture put Anna at ease and gave her confidence for the part the Lord asked her to play today in the Great Commission.

"Emma, we are so happy you are feeling ok and that you and the baby are fine," Anna began.

"Thanks, Anna," Emma replied.

"But, there is another reason for our visit," Anna shared.

"What is that?" Emma asked inquisitively.

"You have not shared a great deal about your life or your circumstances. I want you to know that I am here for you," Anna promised. "To talk, to cry, to listen, or just give a hug."

"Me too, Emma," Rebecca vowed. "Anytime, day or night."

"You are so kind," Emma said choking up from their sentiment.

"Emma, there is also another source of comfort, love, and strength available to you," Anna explained.

Well, his name ain't Jake!"

"No, it is not Jake," Anna confirmed. "Actually, no *man* or *any* human being for that matter can match the source I am speaking of."

Emma listened closely, wanting and needing this information.

"You see, Emma," Anna continued. "We were created intentionally with a longing that can't be filled but one way."

"People try to fill that longing with all sorts of substitutes like alcohol, drugs, or lustful pleasures," Rebecca shared. "They even try to fill that longing with love itself."

"Love? How could love be a wrong choice?" Emma questioned.

"Love is not *wrong*, Emma," Anna clarified. "But human love is not perfect, can't be perfect and therefore human love will not fill that hole, that emptiness deep, deep inside."

"Emma, God is the only one able to fill that longing in your spirit," Rebecca explained. "He created you for His glory and good pleasure. If you could find ultimate satisfaction in earthly substitutes, then you would not need God."

"And He *desires* for you to need Him," Rebecca added. "To seek Him and to find Him."

"And when you find Him, you will find love like none other," Anna shared.

"Well, that sounds amazing," Emma responded.

"You will experience inner joy and peace only when God is first in your life which is His rightful place," Anna continued. "Putting anyone or anything ahead of God is actually a sin called idolatry."

"Like Jake?" Emma asked.

"Yes. I believe Jake is an idol for you," Anna admonished. "But any dependant relationship can be an idol in a person's life."

"I don't feel so good all of a sudden," Emma said and slid down in her bed.

"What is wrong?" Rebecca asked with concern.

"My heart is really racing," Emma said, then blinked her eyes slowly and drew in a deep breath. "And I feel very warm, even sweaty."

Anna knew Emma's condition was spiritual, not physical. "It is the Holy Spirit drawing you to Himself, to have a relationship with God."

"How do I do that?" Emma asked.

"By faith," Rebecca said.

"You see, Emma, God loves you," Anna began. "We are all sinners. In Romans 3:23, the Bible says, *'For all have sinned, and come short of the glory of God.'*"

"No argument there! I have sinned a lot," Emma confessed. "More than I would like to admit."

Anna continued, "Sin separates us from God. In 1 John 1:9, the Bible says, *'If we confess our sins, he is faithful and just to forgive us our sins, and to cleanse us from all unrighteousness.'*"

"God provides a way to restore our relationship with Him. God sent His son Jesus to the earth to pay the price for our sins. Jesus willingly died on a cross, was buried, and after three days rose from the dead and now sits at God's right hand in heaven," Rebecca shared.

"John 3:16 says, *'For God so loved the world, that He gave His only begotten Son, that whosoever believeth in Him should not perish, but have everlasting life,'*" Anna quoted.

"I have heard that scripture before," Emma recalled with excitement in her voice. "But I never really contemplated its meaning until now."

Anna closed, "There is a choice for you to make now. You can choose to spend eternity in heaven with God. Romans 10:9 says, *'That if thou shalt confess with thy mouth the Lord Jesus, and shalt believe in thine heart that God hath raised him from the dead, thou shalt be saved.'*"

"Oh, Anna," Emma exclaimed. "I do believe!"

"Emma, would you like to accept God's free gift of salvation?" Anna asked pointedly.

"YES!" Emma shouted. "YES!"

"Then, Emma, please pray with me now to ask Jesus to live in your heart and be your personal Lord and Savior. Repeat these words out loud and mean them in your heart," Anna instructed.

The room was quiet but for the sing song, back and forth of the following prayer.

"Dear God,

I am sorry for my sins. I believe that Jesus is your son and that He died on a cross to pay for my sins. I believe that He was buried and after three days he rose from the dead. Please forgive me of my sins and save me. Jesus, I ask you to come into my heart and be my personal Savior and the Lord of my life. Holy Spirit, baptize me, fill me to overflowing with your power and love. Father God, I love you and will live for you all the days of my lives.

In Jesus' Name,

Amen."

And the heavens rejoiced as sister Emma joins the family of God!!

39

The waiting room remained crowded even though the time was close to the dinner hour. Abigail and Andrew continued to sleep, seemingly undisturbed by the commotion around them.

Thomas and Matt passed the time swapping stories and sharing their testimonies. Both men thinking that a true friendship was being formed. They were amazed how God used them individually to save a soul. *Maggie's soul.* They were now equally amazed how God was using them to meet another need. Friendship.

Matt and Thomas confessed to one another that they both needed a good guy Christian friend in their lives. Someone to hold the other accountable, someone to whom they could seek Godly counsel, someone to just listen and share a burden or a victory.

Thomas quoted Matthew 6:8, "'....*for your Father knoweth what things ye have need of, before ye ask him.*'"

"So true, my friend," Matt smiled. "So true!"

––––––––––––

Anna and Rebecca stood outside of Emma's door and gave each other a long, firm hug before deciding to part ways for the day. Both women were exhilarated, yet exhausted over the spiritual battle they come through inside while leading Emma to

Christ. Rebecca told Anna of her plans to meet Bonnie in the cafeteria, but she promised to call her before she left the hospital, to be sure that Anna did not need her help that evening.

"Do you think we will be having our sewing class Monday?" Rebecca asked.

"Yes. And I am believing for a full and healthy house full!" Anna spoke in faith.

"I will let Bonnie know," Rebecca said with a huge, bright smile. "See you then, if not before."

"Yes," Anna agreed. "See you! Give Bonnie my love."

"Will do!"

Just as Rebecca turned and headed off, Anna called out, "Rebecca, wait!"

Rebecca spun around, "Yes?"

Thank you," Anna said in a very serious tone. "Thank you for coming today."

"Of course," Rebecca replied.

"Rebecca, before you go, I really want you to know how very valuable your willingness to come and minister today was to advancing the kingdom of God."

"I am glad I could help."

"The Holy Spirit brought two scriptures to my mind that I want to share with you so you can fully understand your role today," Anna explained.

"Great. Please share them with me."

"The first verse is Ecclesiastes 4:9 *'Two are better than one; because they have a good reward for their labour,'* Anna quoted. "You see, God's design is that working in relation with another is simply more productive. YOU were a part of that design today."

"Wow! That is cool!"

Anna continued, "And the second verse is Ecclesiastes 4:12 *'And if one prevail against him, two shall withstand him; and a threefold cord is not quickly broken.'*"

"What does that mean?" Rebecca questioned.

"Alone, a person can be overtaken. Two is better, but three is best. The Lord being the third strand in the cord," Anna taught.

"I think I understand," Rebecca said. "Team work, right? Like God is our Coach, the Bible is our play book, and we are the players."

Anna smiled at the analogy. "Yes. Team work, indeed!"

"Thanks for taking the time to share that with me," Rebecca said. "I better go. Bonnie is waiting for me."

Anna smiled as she watched Rebecca walk down the hall and exit through the automatic double doors of the maternity ward. She couldn't help, but notice a little skip in Rebecca's step.

Walking in God's will is a natural prelude to a joyful heart, and of course skipping is evidence.

Now Anna was off to the ICU waiting room to sit with Abigail and Andrew Tucker while Matt visited Maggie. Oh, how Anna empathized with the fear the children were experiencing inside their hearts. The empathy was very real. She lost both her parents in a car accident when she was just ten years old. It was 9pm at night when her Aunt Clair came over to their house. The babysitter was reading her a Bible story before tucking her in bed. She even remembered the story. Shadrach, Meshach, and Abednego. Teenagers standing for their God. Later she thought how appropriate that was the story for the night. For minutes later her world would change. And she would need to be brave. Just like Shadrach, Meshach, and Abednego.

Aunt Clair, her mother's older sister, came into her bedroom and waived the baby sitter out into the hall where Anna could hear the whispers, then a gasp, then crying. Then Aunt Clair came into her bedroom, sat on her bed and delivered the blow. "There was an accident. They did not survive. Your mom and dad are in heaven, Anna," Aunt Clair explained. "I am sorry."

The room grew black and the deepest pain came over Anna in an instant. She didn't cry. She did not move. She sat still and numb in her bed. In fact, no feeling of any kind returned for a long time.

Anna went to live with Aunt Clair where she finished high school. Her older brother, the biochemistry major, came home from college for the funeral but was never seen again. Anna heard he had made it big. CEO of a pharmaceutical company. Rumor had it he lived in Pittsburgh, just an afternoon's drive to Dayton. Still she hadn't seen him since the cemetery that dreadful day. She remembered him leaving, seeing the back of his head as he ducked into his fancy new BMW. April 12th this year would be the 54th anniversary of her parent's death.

40

"Thank you for everything Thomas," Matt said solemnly.

"You're welcome, Matt."

"You know, you should come by our home some time for a visit," Matt offered. "Come for dinner."

Thomas smiled and nodded his head, "I would like that very much."

The two men swapped business cards and then shook hands good-bye. Matt sat back down next to his children to wait for Anna's return. Thomas was busy reading Matt's business card as he headed across the room to leave the waiting room.

God is a great connector, Thomas thought as his faith in finding his sister grew. *The great connector.*

Anna saw Matt and the children as soon as she entered the waiting room. She quickly headed their way; she felt pressed to hurry because she had spent more time with Emma than she had estimated to Matt. "I am sorry I am late," Anna said.

"Anna, you are not late. I appreciate you helping," Matt expressed. "Besides, I just spent the last hour or so with the man who found Maggie and called the ambulance. He tracked her down to make sure she was ok."

"That was so kind," Anna commented.

"Yes. A kind act by a kind man," Matt smiled.

Just then, Robert, the desk clerk volunteer broke in, "The visiting hour will begin in 5 minutes. Immediate family, you may begin to line up at the door."

Abigail and Andrew began to stir at the sound of Robert's booming voice. Anna nodded to Matt to indicate for him to take his place in line and to reassure him she would take good care of the children. She sat down in the empty chair, where Matt had been sitting and looked at the precious children as they awoke.

She smiled at them as they made eye contact with her. They smiled back at her with a safe, knowing look in their eyes. Abigail got up out of her chair and climbed into Anna's lap. Anna's heart just melted as she wrapped her arms around the sweet girl. Andrew nudged his head along side Anna's arm and rested in on her shoulder. Anna was glad the children had taken to her so well, but she knew by their affection that they missed their mother, and her touch.

Anna knew she needed to intercede for the children in prayer. She prayed aloud, but soft enough that her words were inaudible to the children as she did not want the request to establish any doubt in their minds about Maggie's condition.

"Lord, thank you for saving Maggie. Please quicken her recovery and hasten her healing. Her babies need her. In Jesus' name, Amen."

Bonnie and Rebecca enjoyed coffees in the cafeteria while catching up on all the day's events, including Emma's salvation. They made a schedule between them to alternate bringing meals to both Maggie and Emma for when they left the hospital. Bonnie would bring meals Monday, Wednesday, and Friday to Maggie and Tuesday, Thursday, Saturday to Emma. Rebecca's schedule was the fitting opposite.

They celebrated all the good news and then prepared to say their good-byes, both tired from the long day. Dusk had fallen and the temperature outside had most likely dropped down into the twenties. Buttoning their coats and securing their hats and gloves, they headed out the hospital doors. They gave big hugs before parting ways. Rebecca headed into the parking lot to find her car while Bonnie waited in line for the valet.

Not paying attention to her step, Rebecca almost tripped trudging over a small snow bank. After regaining her balance, she turned and shouted to Bonnie, "See you in class, Monday!"

"Yes. See you in class!" Bonnie shouted back. "Can't wait!"

At nine o'clock, they decided to call it a day and head home. Anna, Matt, Abigail and Andrew left the ICU area together and slowly headed toward the main lobby and out to their cars. Matt felt an onslaught of guilt as he gave a good-bye nod to the security guard in the parking lot. Though he wanted to stay the night, Matt knew Maggie would want him to go home with the children and tuck them into their own beds. Besides, Abigail really missed their dog, Murphy.

Matt would return first thing in the morning. *Sweet dreams, my love*, Matt thought in his heart. *Sweet dreams.*

41

The guest room was bright and cheery just as Brenda described. Emma was so appreciative of her growing friendship with her co-worker. Not only did Brenda pick her up this morning after she checked out of the hospital, she also offered to let Emma stay with her while she recovered further. Brenda insisted, actually. And down deep, Emma was glad not to go home alone to her empty apartment.

After Emma unpacked her few belongings, she laid down on the twin bed for a quick rest. In just a short while, Brenda's brother, Ken, would be arriving to join them for dinner. At first she thought it would be uncomfortable to dine with her divorce attorney, but then she remembered how Ken was able to put her at ease. She was over due in making a follow up appointment with him and resolved to get a meeting scheduled very soon. Perhaps next week, if Ken had an opening. Jake had certainly moved on, the time had come for Emma to accept that as fact.

"*SUPPER!*" Brenda hollered up the stairs. "Ken's here. Come eat!"

Before Emma headed down, she paused to look in the oval framed mirror that hung above the chest of drawers. "Time to move on too, Emma," she said to her reflection. "Yes, time to move on."

Relieved to have been moved from ICU, Maggie found the standard hospital room a place of solace. The quiet was a sharp contrast to the constant motion of the critical care area where she spent the past week. As she reflected on her stay, she gave thanks to God for saving her life and her soul. She knew her life had changed forever. Saturday, Matt would pick her up for check out and they would begin their new journey. This time with Jesus leading the way!

"Thank you, Lord. Thank you."

After hanging up the phone, Thomas glanced down at his notebook to review the draft of his ad that he just read to the classified sales person at the Dayton Herald. He hoped his sister was a subscriber or at the least that a neighbor or friend would see the ad and give her the information. Thomas was so looking forward to this reunion. There was a lot of explaining to do on his part for leaving all those years ago. And even more explaining as to why he stayed away.

"Lord, please give me a chance to make it up to her, he prayed. *Please Lord, one more chance."*

She felt her cheeks turn bright red as Bonnie stood listening to Henry stammer at asking her out on a date. His lips were moving, but Bonnie was so nervous that her mind was not

258

registering his words. She did pick up on the gist of what he was saying, but she could not believe her ears. *A date? Me?*

Both loyal and tenacious employees, Bonnie and Henry were usually the last ones to leave their office each day. Today, Henry asked to walk Bonnie to her car, and she agreed. They were alone in the parking garage, except for the attendant in the booth at the ground floor entrance.

Though not entirely sure what she was agreeing to, Bonnie said, "Yes, sounds good!"

"Great!" Henry said like a love struck teenager. "I will pick you up next Saturday morning about ten o'clock. I *love* the circus and I am so glad you want to join me!"

"It will be fun!" Bonnie replied, relieved Henry repeated the plan. "I live in Oakwood. 21 Dixon Avenue, just around the bend from Harman Elementary School."

"Beautiful area of town," Henry commented.

"It was my mother's home," Bonnie shared. "I have lived there most of my life."

"Well, I look forward to seeing it then," Henry said. "And I look forward to seeing you."

Bonnie was taken aback by Henry's flirting, but she had to admit she liked the attention. She thought about flirting back, but nothing came to mind. *Out of practice,* she thought to herself.

"See you Saturday," was the only thing she could manage to say. Her heart pounded in her chest with excitement as she opened her car door and slid inside. Henry shut the door for her and gave her a wink goodbye.

Am I ready for a date? *For a relationship?* Bonnie speculated. *Maybe, but definitely not a wink?!*

42

Now that spring was drawing near, Matt was anxious to try out the custom grill in their outdoor kitchen. Not sure how long they would have the privilege of living in this upscale community, Matt wanted his family to experience all its luxuries while they had the chance. He also wanted to share the experience with others who meant a lot to their family.

"Maggie?"

"Yes, dear," she replied, feeling as good as new since the accident.

"Do you feel like entertaining this Saturday evening? Maybe a guest or two for dinner?" Matt asked.

"Oh, yes," Maggie said. "I would like to invite Anna. To thank her for all she has done for us."

"And I would like to invite Thomas," Matt said. "To thank him for all he has done for us."

"Great idea!" Maggie exclaimed. "I will call Anna right away to see if she is free."

Maggie headed to the kitchen to make her call while Matt pulled his cell phone out of his pocket and began dialing. As Maggie picked up the receiver, she paused to take in a life moment. *What a treasure Matt is to me, to our family, to our friends! I love him so!* "Thank you, Lord, for providing this fine man to be my husband! Thank you!"

―――――――――――

"Breathe in. Hold it, hold it," the instructor said. "Let it go slowly. Slowly."

This morning was their final birthing class of the six week session. After Emma's release from the hospital, Rebecca offered to be her partner at the delivery and join her in learning and practicing the breathing techniques and methods.

Emma's due date was fast approaching, and she was really starting to get excited to meet her baby. The nursery was ready, her hospital bag was packed, and Rebecca was on stand by to accompany her for the big day.

"Let's try this position again," the instructor continued. "Ready? Begin. Breathe in……"

As they went through the different motions and sequences, Emma thought to herself how blessed she was to have Rebecca as a friend. In between breaths, Emma shared, "Thank you, Rebecca, for being my partner for the delivery and for taking these classes with me. And for being a great friend."

"Oh, Emma," Rebecca replied. "Thank *you*. It is an honor that you have allowed me to share this experience with you."

"You are welcome," Emma said. "You are very welcome."

Filled with gratitude, Emma offered up a silent prayer of thanksgiving. *Thank you, Lord, for my baby. Thank you for my friends. Thank you for this new chapter in my life. May my every moment bring you honor and glory. In Jesus' name, Amen.*

She could not waiver now. It was too late. At the stroke of five, Bonnie confidently entered her boss's office. Standing at the edge of the long cherry desk, Bonnie announced, "Thank you for this opportunity. But my Father has called me to a different job."

"Huh?" he spoke as he stood and parroted her stance.

"I am going to the mission field. Honduras, to be exact."

"What are you talking about?"

"I will give you a full month notice so you have time to hire and train my replacement."

"Are you serious?

"When the Lord calls, it is best to answer," Bonnie explained.

"How about you answer, NO?!" he grew angry.

"Jonah tried that. And it didn't work so well for him," Bonnie shared with a smile.

All too familiar with his own belly of the fish decisions, he finally relented. "I am proud of you, Bonnie," Mr. Hanson said. "I am *really* proud of you."

"Thank you sir," Bonnie replied as she turned and walked out his office door.

I am proud of you too. The Holy Spirit impressed on her heart from the Lord. *Daughter, I am proud of you.*

"Tonight, we finish up our projects, ladies," Anna announced as she circled the room admiring her students' accomplishments.

"If anyone is not complete by the end of class tonight, just feel free to come over one evening this week to sew things up," Anna shared with a grin.

The women laughed at the intended pun, an obvious camaraderie was felt in the place. Sensing a bitter sweet atmosphere at the thought of parting ways, Anna threw out a suggestion.

"How would you like to meet again next week to celebrate all your hard work?"

"YES!" "YES!" "YES!" "YES!"

"It is unanimous then," Anna counted the votes. "A celebration it will be then!"

Anna watched the busy hands finishing up their work. She was so happy with the progress of the women's sewing skills, but even more happy with their spiritual experiences. The Lord exceeded her every expectation of this endeavor.

"Thank you, Lord. To you be the Glory!"

43

Punctuality was never a problem for Thomas. He prided himself on being on time, or early and tonight was no exception. He parked his car, grabbed the flowers off the front seat and headed to the front door of the Tucker's home. Thomas felt that tonight would be special. If he ever claimed a prophetic gift, the time was now. *God was here. Not near, not close by, right smack dab here.*

Maggie and Matt were so looking forward to their company coming this evening. The house was sparkling clean and smelling fresh. The yard was well manicured with signs of spring bursting everywhere. Flower buds were rearing their heads amidst the wintry lawn that struggled to regain its green color. The outdoor kitchen, which was expected to be the hub of the gathering, looked to be straight off the cover of a design magazine. A hot grill, stone fireplace, trendy furniture, and of course, tiki torches lining the perimeter.

Maggie took one last look around for a final inspection, and then headed off to answer the front door. *"Thank you, Lord, for this home and this opportunity to host some friends. You are so good. SO good! Please bless this evening and the guests. I love YOU! Amen".*

Filled with vibrant color and heart pumping music, the video announcements at Dayton Community Church, would always grab Rebecca's attention. Tonight was no different.

Rebecca loved the midweek service and found that the more often she met with other believers, the richer life seemed to be. She was thankful for the fellowship opportunities that helped her transition and replace the old habits from the bar scene.

One announcement in particular made Rebecca sit up in her chair and take notice. The clip showed people from the congregation being interviewed about their experience in belonging to a life group. *A life group? Hmmm...*

After the video was over, the lights came up throughout the sanctuary as the ushers began passing out cards, row by row. The senior pastor stood center stage to explain more about life groups and the cards being distributed. He said that a life group was a small group of believers that met regularly to share life. They prayed for one another, studied the Bible together, shared in each other's burdens and held one another accountable to live a holy life. He said joining a life group would be one of the best decisions you could ever make in your life.

"Live with no regrets!" he bellowed out. "Check either box. Join or host."

When it was Rebecca's turn to take a card and pass the stack, she leaned forward to grab the pen from the chair pocket in front of her. She listened to the pastor continue as she surveyed her card in hand.

"Hosting a group is especially rewarding, but requires a deeper commitment," he explained. "You see, sometimes people will come to a life group before they would come to a church. They can learn about Jesus and accept Him RIGHT THERE IN LIFE GROUP! If your neighborhood needs Jesus, then let God work through you. Be a host!"

The worship band took the stage while the congregation busily completed their cards and dropped them into the collection buckets as they passed. Check. Rebecca's palms sweated as she checked the host box. Excitement, hope, and purpose filled her heart as she imagined pinning flyers on the dorm bulletin boards. *Where would they meet?   In the lobby, perhaps? A library meeting room? A corner in the student union café? Somewhere on campus would be best, for sure.*

Rebecca's mind raced with ideas, so much so that she intermittently missed the sermon. She jotted down her thoughts as they flooded in, excited for this new adventure. *"Thank you, Lord. Thank you for this church and this opportunity to serve you. Help me to reach the campus for you. FOR YOU! In Jesus' name. Amen.*

Red potatoes, onions, celery, gobs of mayonnaise and of course a pinch of relish. *The family potato salad recipe was sure to please*, Anna thought as she rang the door bell, dish in hand.

"Come in!" Maggie exclaimed. "So glad you could come!!"

"Glad to be here!" Anna replied, hugging Maggie with her spare arm.

While the ladies caught up with each other in the foyer, Matt and Thomas were busy swapping stories and flipping steaks out back. The weather was nice, mid sixties, with a bit of a breeze, a welcome change from the brutal winter. Maggie took Anna on a brief tour of their home before joining the men on the patio.

Matt saw the women approaching the slider and passed his tongs to Thomas so he could help them with the door. "Would you mind?" Matt asked his friend.

"Not at all," Thomas said. "It's been awhile, but I think I can manage."

Thomas's back was toward the door when Anna and Maggie stepped on the deck. Matt and Maggie exchanged a quick smooch on the lips.

"Hi honey," Matt greeted his wife, then turned to Anna. "Hello, Anna. So glad you could make it!"

"Hello, Matt. I wouldn't have missed it. Thanks for having me," Anna replied.

Thomas was focusing on the steaks, but couldn't help but notice that the guest's name was Anna. *My sister's name is Anna.* He hesitated before turning around and decided to wait for Matt to make an introduction. *Her voice. Familiar, yet not quite.*

"Thomas!" Matt called out. "THOMAS!" he raised his voice over the sizzle of the grill.

As Thomas turned around, his eyes instantly locked on Anna's. *No introduction necessary.*

Matt and Maggie sensed at once that something unusual was happening. These two strangers knew each other. But how?

Bzzz. Bzzz. Rebecca felt the vibration of her cell phone over and over in her purse. After the third set of rings, Rebecca reached in and retrieved her phone to see who was being so persistent.

The display showed three missed calls and one text.

She quickly clicked view message.

"It's time!"

Anna felt light headed at the first realization that she was standing face to face with her brother. A series of emotions ran quickly through her being. Within seconds, she experienced anger, then sadness, then joy. Anger for his leaving, sadness for his stubborn distance, and joy for his return.

"Sister!" Thomas said as he laid the tongs on a side counter and walked slowly toward his sibling.

269

With tears pouring down her cheeks, Anna walked toward him with her arms stretched out wide.

"Brother!"

They hugged and held each other tight. Matt and Maggie stood in amazement, not sure what to do next. But then, in the midst of the embrace, both Maggie and Anna's cell phones began to ring. Anna was oblivious, content in her brother's arms. Maggie acted quickly in hopes of not disrupting the moment. She dug her phone from her pocket and read the new text. It was from Rebecca.

Maggie took a short gasp of air before a huge smile spread across her face. "Anna," Maggie whispered softly. She knew Anna would want to know the news.

Anna opened her eyes and looked at Maggie, her head continuing to rest on her big brother's shoulder.

Maggie mouthed to her, "It's time!" She repeated, "It's time!"

Brenda got the text at the hotel where she was working the second shift at the front desk. Immediately, she slipped from behind the counter and poked her head into her boss's office. "It's time!" Brenda shared with a big smile, holding the screen of her cell phone to show Kathy how she heard the news.

"Go!" Kathy ordered. "I'll cover the rest of the evening."

Brenda quickly texted back to Emma that she was on the way.

"Thank you for covering!"

"No problem," Kathy replied. "Call me later."

"Will do!" Brenda promised as she grabbed her purse and pulled on her jacket. As she rushed out the main door to the parking garage, she felt honored to be Emma's designated driver. *On my way, friend. On my way.*

A quiet night at home was Bonnie's plans for this spring evening. There were lots to do before she left for Honduras. She still couldn't believe she finally had her boss's permission, or at least his tolerance, for this mission trip. Rather than quitting her job entirely, her boss convinced her to take a leave of absence. For the sake of peace, Bonnie agreed to his terms, figuring her fate was in her Father's hands anyhow.

She had grabbed a few cardboard boxes at the grocery store on her way home from the office. Her idea was to pack and store her things in a storage unit while she was away. Her lease was up in thirty days anyway, so it would be more economical for her to pay rent on a storage unit than on her apartment. *Still an accountant*, she chuckled as she crunched the numbers in her head.

Just as she began to load up her first box with knick-knacks and what-knots, she heard her cell phone buzz. She laid the wrapping paper aside and headed to her purse to retrieve her phone. A creature of habit, probably another accountant trait, Bonnie always kept her phone in the same spot, her purse. Easy, predictable, routine.

"It's time," read the text from Rebecca.

44

By the time they arrived at Dayton General, they had learned from Rebecca that Emma was already admitted into the hospital and soon on her way to being a mother. Anna, Thomas, Maggie and Matt rode together in the Tucker's vehicle, all committed to staying the night if need be. Matt's older sister, Elizabeth, came over in a moment's notice to sleep over and babysit her niece and nephew.

As they approached the maternity ward waiting room, Anna spotted Rebecca exiting the double doors of the delivery area. Her concern faded as she saw the reassuring smile on Rebecca's face.

"Hi everyone!" she practically shouted.

Greetings came from everywhere as Bonnie and Brenda joined in from down the hall.

"What did I miss?" Brenda asked. "I just took a quick walk. I was too nervous to sit and wait."

"How is Emma?" inquired Bonnie.

"Emma is just fine," Rebecca shared relieving the tension. "She wanted me just to come out and thank you all for being here."

"Well, of course," Anna comforted. "Send in our love."

"We will be praying," Maggie added.

"I better go," Rebecca said. "It won't be long now!"

Anna and Thomas broke away for a private conversation while they walked a nearby hall, staying close enough in case there was news. .

Matt and Maggie sat in adjacent chairs, hand in hand, quiet and still. So comfortable with each other they almost needed no words.

Bonnie and Brenda sat opposite the Tuckers and chit chatted about everything from chewing gum to pocket calculators and anything in between.

"Push, Emma, push!" Rebecca coached on as she dabbed the sweat from Emma's brow. "You are almost there!"

"AHHHHH," groaned Emma pushing with all her might, as she grit her teeth and reared up in the bed. "ERRRRR!"

———

Lucas's cheeks were rosy, picture perfect. His brown black hair was piled high on top of his head. His face was round with a deep dimple in the middle of his chin. His lips were just like Emma's, no doubt about that. Healthy and happy, weighing in at eight pounds, six ounces, young Luke entered the world at 10:04pm, May 28th.

Emma and Rebecca both cried tears of joy as they marveled at this miracle. Swaddled tight in the standard white and blue stripped cotton blanket, Emma cradled her newborn snuggly in her arms. She turned to Rebecca to try and explain what she was feeling inside. "God surprised me!"

"How do you mean?" Rebecca asked.

"I prayed and prayed for a healthy baby and a safe delivery," Emma said. "He answered that prayer."

"Halleluiah!" Rebecca rejoiced. "But, what is the surprise?"

"He is beautiful. Just beautiful," Emma said. "I prayed for the baby's health, never beauty. It was a surprise!"

"God is good!"

"AMEN!"

———————

At Emma's request, Rebecca left her friend's side to go gather up those waiting to meet little Luke. Meanwhile, Anna, Maggie, Bonnie, Brenda, Matt and Thomas had remained in the waiting room enjoying their time together while anticipating the arrival of Emma's baby.

Rebecca's heart was bursting with excitement when she opened the waiting room door and made the announcement. Cheers broke out instantly as the friends jumped to their feet and exchanged hugs and high fives.

"Oh, such wonderful news!" Anna exclaimed, folding her hands and lifting her eyes to the heavens. *"Thank you, Lord, for this new life!"*

"Emma would like to see you," Rebecca shared. "Yes. ALL of you!"

They looked at each other and nodded in agreement, then cheerfully followed Rebecca back to Emma's room. Ooo's and aah's filled the room as each person took a turn peeking at Emma's sweet baby. Emma's smile could not have been brighter and her countenance never more peaceful.

"Anna, would you pray?" Emma asked humbly.

Instinctively, the friends formed a circle around Emma's bed and joined hands. Anna stood closet to Emma and laid her free hand on Emma's shoulder.

"Heavenly Father, we gather here today to celebrate life and love. We thank you for the birth of this precious child, Lucas, and for seeing our sister Emma safely through her delivery. We thank you for dear friends and family. Most of all we are thankful for you. For the very gift of life itself. For every breath we take is by your grace. Bless Lucas with good health, long life, and loving relationships. May he fulfill all the plans and purposes you have laid out for him. May he come to know you personally at the very earliest possible age. Bless Emma and equip her to raise this baby boy into a Godly man. And Father God,, tug on the hearts in this room to be a community of love and support for Emma, to assist her in bringing up Lucas in the church and in your Word. Hold us accountable this day. We love you. It is in Jesus' name we pray. Amen."

45

Baby Luke was the center of attention at the class finale. Emma had only been home from the hospital a few days, but insisted on making tonight's celebration. Anna offered to push the plans back a week, but Emma was set in her decision.

Instead of the sewing room, the ladies gathered in the cozy den for this evening's festivities. Anna explained that the agenda for the night was to show their work and what their finished piece meant to them.

Rebecca went first. "Well, this is my tote bag." She held it up high and moved it from left to right over her head before returning it to her lap. "It is large. It is sturdy. And it can hold a lot," she began. "When I started this class, my life was full. Full of worries, cares, and problems! Then a few months back, I accepted Jesus as my Savior. I surrendered my life to Him AND all my cares." Rebecca turned her tote bag upside down showing it was empty inside. "This tote is like my life. When I cast my cares on Jesus, he carries my burdens, not me."

The ladies smiled in agreement. Bonnie went next showing her comforter, moving it side to side in the same fashion as Rebecca's display. "This is my comforter. It *comforts* me, like its namesake." She laid it across her lap and then raised it up chin level seeming to demonstrate how she would use it in her very own bed. "When I began this class, my life was abysmal. I turned to food for comfort. I did not honor my body, and I did not honor the Lord. But He got my attention. Shortly after my heart attack, I accepted Jesus as my Savior. Now His Holy Spirit is my comforter. My project reminds me of that promise. This comforter is special to me. You are all special to me. And so is my new life with the Lord."

"Oh, thank you, Bonnie," Anna said. "Who's next?"

"I'll go," Maggie replied. She held up a stack of beautiful linen place mats with her right hand, and matching napkins with her left. After the women got a good look, she set them back down on her lap. There was a moment of silence before she began, so tender was her salvation.

"When I started this class, my family and I were residents at the Chrysalis Center for the Homeless, a result of my husband, Matt, losing his job, which rolled into the foreclosing of our family home." Gasps filled the room as the women were unaware of the Tucker's plight. "These table linens represented hope to me. They allowed me to dream. To dream of a dining table, in our own home, with my family seated together sharing meals." Maggie choked back tears. "After my car accident, my husband shared with me how he had recommitted his life to Christ. And that his new job and our new home were all blessings from the Lord. I accepted Jesus as my Savior. I now trust Him for our provision. My project represents hope. And Jesus is the one true hope."

The ladies clapped their hands after Maggie's presentation. "Thank you, Maggie," Anna said. "Thank you for sharing."

Then Anna stood and walked toward Emma offering to hold Luke while she showed her project. "May I?" she asked, cradling her open arms toward the new mom.

"Oh, yes," Emma agreed and gently passed her sweet son. Anna smiled as she gazed at Luke sleeping, all swaddled up in his baby blue blanket.

"Well, when I started this class, I was a wreck. Confused, lonely, guilt-ridden, and depressed. But, inside of me grew this *life*. I knew that if I could hold onto the thought of new life, I could make it." Emma rubbed her tummy thinking back to those days.

"This is my baby blanket." She paused and held up her blanket to the others, then folded it up and placed it on it on top of Luke's car seat. "With each class, with each stitch, I came closer to my baby. I came closer to new life."

Looking over at Luke, she continued. "My reaction to seeing Jake that day and the feelings that pushed me to that emotional state were life changing. At my breaking point, I accepted Jesus as my Savior. My blanket reminds me of my baby. It also reminds me of newness of life, both birth and *re*birth. The miracle of birth, the gift of rebirth. Luke is new and I am new."

The women stood and gathered close, embracing one another in a circle of friendship and love. Tears flowed as the realization of their final class became real.

"Your projects are beautiful creations. YOU are beautiful creations." Anna looked into the eyes of each woman individually. "Remember the promise in 2 Corinthians 5:17, *'Therefore if any man be in Christ, he is a new creature: old things are passed away; behold, all things are become new.'*"

The women repeated the scripture in unison, proclaiming truth and freedom.

Anna shared a final word, "The Bible says in Psalm 107:2, *'Let the redeemed of the Lord say so...'*" She paused, and gave her last instruction. "Say so! Tell your story to others of how Jesus made *you* a new creation. May the Lord use your testimony to bring souls into the Kingdom of God. Say so! Say so! Say so!"

The twinkle in Emma's eye sparked a near revival right there on Albert Street. She turned and took hold of her baby blanket and raised it high in the center of the circle as if giving a toast. "Say SEW!"

The ladies laughed and followed her lead, lifting their projects and joining her in the toast.

"Say SEW! Say Sew! Say SEW!"

EPILOGUE

God loves you.

We are all sinners. The Bible says, *"For all have sinned, and come short of the glory of God."* **Romans 3:23**

Sin separates us from God. The Bible says, *"If we confess our sins, he is faithful and just to forgive us our sins, and to cleanse us from all unrighteousness."* **1 John 1:9**

God provides a way to restore our relationship with Him. God sent His son Jesus to the earth to pay the price for our sins. Jesus willingly died on a cross, was buried, and after three days rose from the dead and now sits at God's right hand in heaven. *"For God so loved the world, that He gave His only begotten Son, that whosoever believeth in Him should not perish, but have everlasting life."* **John 3:16**

There is a choice for you to make now. You can choose to spend eternity in heaven with God. The Bible says, *"That if thou shalt confess with thy mouth the Lord Jesus, and shalt believe in thine heart that God hath raised him from the dead, thou shalt be saved."* **Romans 10:9**

New Life

If you would like to accept God's free gift of salvation, please pray the following prayer to ask Jesus to live in your heart and be your personal Lord and Savior.

Dear God,

I am sorry for my sins. I believe that Jesus is your son and that He died on a cross to pay for my sins. I believe that He was buried and after three days he rose from the dead. Please forgive me of my sins and save me. Jesus, I ask you to come into my heart and be my personal Savior and the Lord of my life. Holy Spirit, baptize me, fill me to overflowing with your power and love. Father God, I love you and will live for you all the days of my lives.

In Jesus' Name, Amen

STUDY GUIDE

Session 1, Chapters 1-10

1. Which character do you relate to best? Why?_____

_____

_____

_____

_____

_____

_____

_____

2. Which character best describes someone you love? Or someone you find difficult to love? Why?_____

_____

_____

_____

_____

_____

_____

_____

Memory Verse:
Luke 1:37 *"For with God nothing shall be impossible."*

Session 2, Chapters 11-20

Review of Memory Verse:
Luke 1:37 *"For with _____ _____ shall be _____."*

1. Keeping with the character who *you* relate to best, describe how God is moving in their life? _____

   _____

   _____

   _____

   _____

   _____

   _____

   _____

2. Describe one way God has revealed Himself to you? _____

   _____

   _____

   _____

   _____

   _____

   _____

   Memory Verse:
   Philippians 4:13 *"I can do all things through Christ who strengthenth me."*

Session 3, Chapters 21-30

Review of Memory Verse:
Phillipians 4:13 "*I* ____ *do* ____ *things through* _____ *who strengthenth* ____."

1. Again, keeping with the character who *you* relate to best, identify what you believe to be their greatest struggle in life? _____

   _____

   _____

   _____

   _____

   _____

2. Describe *your* greatest struggle in life?

   _____

   _____

   _____

   _____

   _____

   _____

Memory Verse:
Romans 12:2 *"And be not conformed to this world: but be ye transformed by the renewing of your mind, that ye may prove what is that good, and acceptable, and perfect, will of God."*

Review of Memory Verse:
Romans 12:2 *"And be _____ conformed to this*
_____: but be ye _____ by the
_____ of your mind, that ye may prove
what is that good, and acceptable, and
_____, _____ of God."

1. Once again, studying the character
   who *you* relate to best, describe how
   he/ she responds to the Gospel message.

   _____

   _____

2. *Why* do you think he/ she responds that
   way? _____

   _____

   _____

Homework to bring to Session 5:
Write your personal testimony on the following
page. Be prepared to share before your group at
the next session. Please include the events
leading up to your salvation and how you came
to make your decision. Be specific. How did
God draw you? What has life been life as a born
again Christian?

If you do NOT have a salvation testimony, please
see your group leader for further information.

Session 5, Chapters 41-45

Psalms 107:2 *"Let the redeemed of the Lord say so….."*

My Testimony

_____

_____

_____

_____

_____

_____

_____

_____

_____

_____

_____

_____

_____

To share your testimony, or to contact Stephanie for speaking engagements, please email:
stephanieconnors@outlook.com

To order more copies of <u>Sew Sisters</u>, *please visit:*
www.stephanieconnors.org

www.ingramcontent.com/pod-product-compliance
Lightning Source LLC
Chambersburg PA
CBHW070838250626
47159CB00003B/836